A CHILD GOES MISSING

Written by Mary Jane Carter

ISBN 9781536581829

Acknowledgment

This book is dedicated to my family, whose love and support mean more to me than anything else in the world.

CHAPTER ONE

Present Day

The key to making the perfect kill is to line up your prey *and then squeeze* the trigger. Wow! What a rush to make a fresh kill. Killing is what I do. It is the only thing that I am truly gifted at in this world. The most common mistake most people make when hunting, is that they see their prey and pull the trigger. Pulling the trigger causes the gun to jerk slightly to the side. That jerk, imperceptible to the shooter, begins a chain reaction that over the distance between the shooter and the prey the shot is a complete miss. The shooter is mystified at the miss never knowing that it is all because they pulled the trigger instead of squeezing it. I have seen some fools get lucky. They just point and shoot willy-nilly and get their prey, but it is not a deliberate act of seek, conquer and destroy. By squeezing the trigger, the same amount of pressure is applied evenly keeping the gun stable through the whole shot. Bam, you get the perfect shot. Perfect shot equals the perfect kill. This is my talent. I can shot a target up to a quarter a mile away and even further on a clear no wind day. I am what they call the fixer. I solve problems permanently. I never miss.

I line up my sight and peer through. There's my target. I can feel the adrenaline pumping and I inhale deeply. The adrenaline helps with the high of a fresh kill, but can also interfere with the mechanics of the shot. A deep breath exhaled slowly will steady the physical nature of the task. Wait for the eyes, wait for the target to look you in the eyes. Some days you have to almost coax your prey to look at you. Through the sight the prey feels like they are right next to you. Wait for it. Look at me. Come on baby look at papa. The target turns and stares on cue, she stares right down the barrel of the gun. The shot makes a hissing sound as it leave the gun due to the silencer. I like using a silencer, but not for the reason one might expect. I simply enjoy the sound of the silencer. It is the sound of a lethal snake, hiss, just as it is about to strike. Of course, I get the added bonus of not having to wear hearing protection, and that means I can hear what is happening in my immediate surroundings. For some people, making the kill gives them an adrenaline rush, I call it a dump when all the adrenaline pours through the system at once. These dumps allow for incredible feats of strength and then the rush is over. For me, I get a slow stream of adrenaline that starts the moment I plan my kill. Each phase adds to the steady stream of adrenaline building to a crescendo with the kill. The high from the adrenaline can last me days even weeks depending on how challenging the set up and take down was.

This particular kill required shooting at some distance, not a career maker, but a longer shot than most. In the past, long shots were risky, but with all the adaptations for hunters on the market even an idiot can make a shot. With the right equipment, all you had to do these days was site the shot dial in the numbers and squeeze the trigger. If more people had the stomach for my line of work, I could easily find myself out of a job. Thankfully, most people do not have the constitution and simply cannot do what I do.

This kill was clean, right in the forehead the target dropped instantly. Site, squeeze, hiss, and drop. Next comes the waiting. Wait to see if there is an alarm, reaction, witnesses, anything at all that could challenge the kill. This is where most people make a critical mistake. They don't wait to see the reaction and respond accordingly. They always panic and get out too quickly and leave behind critical career ending evidence. But then again, they are not professional killers like me.

I wait and watch, no movement from anywhere, no alarms. Next comes the packing up and exit. Packing up my rifle takes me less than ten seconds. I back out of the room to make sure I don't miss anything or worse, leave something behind. Backing out of a crime scene makes it almost impossible for anyone to walk up from behind you. Finally, the exit, I need to get away without raising so much as an eyebrow. This requires a calm and controlled exit. No running, no panic, just a purposeful walk to your getaway.

They will call the local law enforcement when they discover the body. Around here the local law enforcement has the minimal investigative training and no more. This time of year the local cops will blame it on hunters. This will never be classified as anything other than a hunting accident. Investigating this shooting would require work and people are generally lazy, especially small town cops. Given a credible explanation of a hunting accident, the police will look no further. Laziness and habits make my work so easy. Take picking the kill location, one look at the bartender and I knew she would be too lazy to check the upstairs before locking up for the night.

Sometimes, I staked out my target for weeks before the kill. I look for a pattern in their daily life and fit the kill into natural surroundings. This one was easy, early autumn in the North Woods of Maine. This one was practically dictated to me, a hunting accident. My signature kill was to make it look like an accident. Rarely, were any of my kills investigated beyond the initial ruling of the death as accidental. This kill took me less than three days, a personal record. My target was in the habit of getting to work early. She would arrive before anyone else meaning that there would be no witness, no instant emergency calls, and time for me to make an exit. She was in the habit of drinking her coffee by the window creating the perfect shot. The light from her office framed her face well in the window. The cops would suspect a rifle shot, they may even recover the bullet and rule this death an unfortunate hunting accident. No one around here will challenge the report, not her friends or family. This is small town America and nothing torrid happens in small town America.

CHAPTER TWO

September – Two months earlier

T he overhead bedroom lights snap on, flooding the room in light. Casey bolts upright startled with a sense impending urgency, which instantly changes when she sees the smiling face of Georgia.

"Peek-A-Boo Mom Mom, " Georgia sings out as she climbs into bed.

"Good morning my love." Casey watches her daughter as she snuggles down in bed lying right next to her. Her daddy and I call her a heat-seeking missile the way she plasters her body right up against you. Three years old and I still cannot believe she is here, and she is mine.

Some mornings Georgia crawls into bed and fall right back to sleep, this is not going to be one of those morning. Georgia's eyes were wide open, and she is telling her mother about all her imaginary friends. Casey marvels at Georgia's vocabulary and imagination. Unfortunately, Casey did not know any other three-year-olds and had no frame of reference to gauge if her daughter was advanced or not. *Just so long as she is happy and healthy, everything else is icing on the cake. To think we almost never had her, and now she is here, this amazing sweet angel.*

"Can I watch *Julius Jr.*?" Georgia asks sweetly batting her eyes something that at the age of three she had mastered quite well when she wants something.

"I don't know Hun. We have to see what is on the TV. What are we having for breakfast?" As both mother and daughter get out of bed heading towards the living room.

"Oh, I want *Julius Jr.*!" Georgia believes her Mom is all-powerful and able to do anything including programming the TV at whim.

"Julius Jr. for breakfast? I don't think we have any of that." Casey switched the conversation knowing that any cartoon on TV would make Georgia happy.

"Noooo!" Georgia giggled. "I want banana yogurt. I love banana yogurt."

Casey turns on the TV and tuned in Nickelodeon, *Julius Jr.* was just starting. *Amazing, this kid is tuned into everything.*

Casey opened up a container of banana yogurt and sets it in front of Georgia and kisses her daughter on the top of the head.

"Thank you Mom Mom. I love you."

"I love you too." Georgia goes into the bedroom and said to her husband, Tom. "You're up, she is eating yogurt watching TV, and I'm going to jump in the shower." Casey kisses Tom and disappears into the bathroom.

"Aren't you going for a run?" Tom called after his wife.

"I got an early meeting with Sally." Casey yells over the sound of the shower.

Casey lets the hot water penetrate all the pores of her body letting that last bit of sleep wash down the drain. Mentally prepping for her day, Casey reviews her classes and the lesson plans as she washes her hair. She considers the questions she will pose to her students to provoke a heated debate. Casey gave the impression of being a teacher that taught in the moment, but most of the time Casey planned her lessons to be provocative and engaging. Casey enjoyed challenging her students to think by creating highly controversial discussions and picking the unpopular side for herself. The strategy is to get students engaged by picking a highly charged topic encouraging students challenging her authority as adult and teacher in a manner that is meaningful and productive. Casey hope was to produce a generation of thinkers that would challenge the establishment when necessary by being highly informed critical thinkers.

The hot water felt great and Casey wanted a few more minutes, but she really did have to get going. She turns the water full blast to cold to get a final wake-up jolt. It works. Casey quickly dried and dressed. She was not in the habit of wearing makeup and quickly twisted her hair up in a bun secured with a hair clip.

The fall colors have just past their peak and Casey smells the distinct odor of snow in the air. Most people don't know that snow has its own smell, but when you first recognize it you never forget the smell of snow. Not entirely unusual to have snow this early, but that could mean a very long winter. It also meant that they needed to "put the wood up" earlier than usual. Putting the wood up, meant stacking the wood in a place that you could get to it all winter long. Most years this task was completed over the long Thanksgiving Holiday. *Looks like we'll be starting it this weekend.* In all honesty, Casey enjoyed the hard manual labor that came with living in rural Maine. Most of the work was physically hard, but mindless, and it allowed her just to be in the moment to reflect and was good for her health too.

CHAPTER THREE

*L*ife doesn't get any better than this thought Jane as she held her granddaughter. Just then the little baby girl looked right into her grandmother's eyes and Jane swore she smiled. *I never knew I could feel such love.* Jane beamed at the new baby cooing and smiling. Jane thought back to the day she first held her daughter Carolyn, never imagining that one day she would be holding her granddaughter. Carolyn was adopted and very much loved, but the process of adoption takes away the anticipation of pregnancy. Jane was not present when Carolyn was born, never met the birth parents, and did not know of any prenatal care. Carolyn had been a private adoption that Jane had paid an agency a lot of money to deliver her a baby. It was more like going shopping for a kid instead of having a baby. This baby she held in her arms was different. From the moment that Jane found out Carolyn was expecting she had waited for this moment, dreamed of it, worried about it. I have imagined a thousand lives for this little one. This was even sweeter than getting Carolyn.

The smell of her granddaughter was intoxicating. Inhaling her was akin to inhaling life. Her fair tuft of hair on the top of her head reminded her of an angel's feather. Jane could not take her eyes off the creamy complexion and the slight blush to her cheeks. Every part of her was perfect from her tiny eyelashes to her little toenails. For the first time ever, she understood the phrase that children were a miracle from God. "You will want for nothing. You will be loved and cherished until the day you die," whispered Jane into her granddaughter's ear. Humming and rocking, Jane held this amazing creature in her arms. She did not feel this overwhelming sense of love when Carolyn was given to her. *I was so young and scared when we got Carolyn, but this beauty. This beauty is all mine.* Jane's heart was so full of love she thought it might actually explode.

Reluctantly Jane gave her granddaughter back to Carolyn. "Carolyn, you have outdone yourself. She is amazing."

Carolyn beamed holding her daughter in her arms. Her mother, Jane had never been an overly emotional person or one to give out praise, so it was odd to witness this outpour of emotion and flattery from her mother.

"Thank you, mom, you're the best. I hope I am half the mom you were." Carolyn said these words to appease her mother, but deep down Carolyn prayed that she would show her daughter all the love she felt for her and not hide it away as Jane had always done with her.

"You already are." Jane kissed her daughter promising to be waiting for her at the house tomorrow. Jane knew that she was often a cold, demanding woman. She had been particularly demanding of Carolyn. Jane wondered if Carolyn knew the depths of her love for her even though she did not always show it. She wanted Carolyn to be strong and capable, but Jane regretted not having more fun with Carolyn when she was growing up. Jane was always afraid that she would lose Carolyn, that one day someone would come and take her away. She had a recurring nightmare that Carolyn's biological parents would one day show up and claim her. Then when Jane learns the whole truth about Carolyn's adoption, her nightmares became daily anxiety attacks. The fear was so intense, Jane never told Carolyn that she was adopted and forbade her husband from telling his daughter the truth. That last thing she wanted was for Carolyn to start looking for her biological parents.

Jane felt the vibrations of her phone. Instinct told her to ignore the call, but she did not ignore calls. She pulled the phone out of her pocket, but did not recognize the number. *I don't talk to telemarketers either* she said to herself and let the call go to voice mail.

Walking arm and arm out to the car with her husband, Jane, felt the vibration of her phone again. She slipped the phone out of her pocket and knew it was the same caller even before she saw the unfamiliar number. *I might as well get this over with, so they don't keep calling all day.* She answered and heard a familiar voice.

"Congratulations on your granddaughter." The phone went dead.

Jane felt a chill up her spine and stopped walking. Something in the voice told her that everything she treasured was in danger.

"What is it?" You're shaking." Her husband asked with masked fear.

"It's nothing." She shook her shoulders to get rid of the feeling of dread. "Just a busy day and I haven't eaten anything." She tried to smile, but she knew the smile was phony. Her husband knew she was putting on a brave face and placating, but did not challenge her. Just pulled her in a little closer sending the message that she always had him to lean on, no matter what.

CHAPTER FOUR

The warning sound was a "ping" that grabbed David's attention, he had never heard it before, but he knew it was an alarm of sorts. Immediately David looked up trying to locate the source of the noise. David realized that the source was coming from his own computer terminal. David had been working for the Senator for almost two years, and this had never heard the computer make this noise before. David rolled his chair over to in front of the computer and read the flashing warning sign. The computer had never done anything like this before either except when it was about to nose dive into a fatal cyber meltdown.

David tapped on the keyboard, but the screen kept flashing the word *warning*. Oh, *No, No, No, No, don't crash on me.* David tried to hit the escape button, but the computer did not respond. David hit the function keys on the top row, but the warning sign continued. David hit the function keys with the control key one at a time. Nothing. The last time David had seen a warning sign the computer's hard drive crashed, and he lost every bit of data. It had taken him months to recreate all of his work. Since then he was much better at backing up his data, but the thought of losing another computer made David anxiety go through the roof. David looked at his hands and could see them shaking ever so slightly.

David stopped to think what he should do. Maybe it was a glitch in the system and decided to kill the power. Just like resetting his Wi-Fi at home, disconnect the power and wait to the count of ten. David always waited more than the count of ten, just to be safe. *Nine, Ten, Eleven, Twelve...* David turned on the system. Nothing happened.

David started to panic when the system kicked in, and the login screen appeared. The thought of calling Technical Support made David's skin crawl. Those guys always made him feel stupid usually asking if the computer was turned on. David had not logged into the system in a long time and was not sure he could remember his password. David rummaged in the top drawer of the desk to find the yellow sticky note he wrote his username and password. The sticky note was plaster to the bottom of the desk under everything. David typed in his username and password. Invalid username and password printed across the screen returning David to the login page. David tried it again. David read the same message as before with the added message that three failed attempts would lock out the user and suggest calling the System Administrator for assistance. David sat back frustrated, he did not know why his username and password were not working, and he did not want to be locked out of the system. He should not have killed the power to the system. David then remembered that this was not his computer, it had been swapped out last week with the Senator's desktop. David held his breath and tried again if this didn't work he'd have to call the Tech guys anyways. David keyed in the Senator's first initial and last name for the username and 1lov3Ma1n3, *I love Maine with changing the letters "i" and "e" to numbers.* Bingo! After almost two years, he did know something about the woman he worked for he smiled to himself feeling like he had just achieved a major accomplishment. The Senator never worked here and so there was nothing sensitive on her computer, so David inherited her computer.

The warning sign started flashing again. David was frustrated and slapped his hand on the keyboards and the warning sign stopped flashing and the name *Special Agent Timothy Thibodeau Bangor Office 207-947-6670* began scrolling across the screen. David stared at the words confused he read along mouthing the words at the moved across the computer screen. *Special Agent Timothy Thibodeau Bangor Office 207-* when the lights went out. The computer screen faded to the center of the screen with a single pinpoint of light then went black. The inner office had no outside windows and went dark, no lights, the phones dead. David stepped out in the hallway and saw the emergency lights on. Several other office workers were emerging into the hallway indicating the entire building was without power. The others in the hallway looked around with questioning looks on their faces and began to mingle inquiring if anyone knew the source of the power outage. Some shrugged their shoulders and returned to their offices, other milled around and talked to one another. David returned to the office and sat down at his desk, after two years he still did not have any friends at work. Power outages happened all the time in Maine, but not to government buildings as a matter of fact David could not recall a single time the power went out in this building. The whole building is supposed to be on a back up generator so the government can run no matter what. David sat there and waited in the dark for the lights to come on.

CHAPTER FIVE

C asey entered Sally's office and grabbed a cup a coffee and some coffee cake. "You know the only reason I agree to these early morning meetings is because you always have the good stuff." Casey licked the sugar off her fingers smiling.

"Who are we drinking from today?" Sally inquired. Sally had an amazing collection of college coffee mugs. One from every college she either visited or placed a student. Over the years, Sally had quite a collection, it was the guidance counselor' version of a glory wall.

"Bates." Casey poked fun. "A bit of the macabre." Bates College always made her think of Norman Bates and the movie Psycho.

"Good choice." Sally said raising her own coffee mug as a toast.

Casey liked and respected Sally which was saying a lot because since moving to this town she had pretty much come to think quite poorly of the moral constitution of most people that lived here, drug addicts and child molesters. The kids around here hardly had a chance with parents like this, but Sally gave one hundred percent to her students every day without getting soured or jaded. To Sally's credit she had placed most students in college and even had one go to Harvard.

"So, early morning meeting. What did you want to talk about?" Casey started.

"We have a new family moving in and I want to place the oldest daughter in your class."

"That's fine, you always dump the transfer students on me. What's different this time?"

"I don't know." Sally shook her head. "I can't put my finger on it, but when I met with the mother and daughter something was wrong. All my alarm bells went off. I think it will be a rough transition and an unwelcomed one on the part of the daughter."

"Okay, but you know that I teach Consumer Economics, not Miracle Making 101." Casey teased.

"Ah, but miracles are what you always seem to do. Remember Jess?" Sally arched her eyebrows lifting her coffee mug once again.

"Right, like I am going to forget Jess, she is over at my house at least once a week. She's a good kid with rotten parents, let's say, Tom and I can relate." *Jess is a good kid with really messed up parents. Jess put in all the hard work, got her high school diploma, earned a full ride to the University of Maine. She just needed a push, and she made me look like teacher of the year.*

"Remember Matt?" Sally asked.

"Okay, I get it. I'm a sucker. Anything I should know? Anything I can use?" Casey asked in feigned surrender.

"Nothing, I got nothing."

CHAPTER SIX

Theresa Rowe had just moved to Redwood with her mother. They rented a small house right in town. The landlord lived in the house behind them, and he gave Theresa the creeps. Theresa complained about the landlord to her mother, and her mother responded that everyone gave Theresa the creeps. *Only the ones you hang out with,* Theresa thought to herself. The last year living with her mother had been difficult. Her mother's drug use was out of control. Every night was a party with a parade of men in and out of the house. Theresa was becoming increasingly afraid to go home. She was never sure what she would find. Would her mother be there? Would her mother be high? Her mother had spent a lot of her childhood in drug rehabilitation centers and during those times Theresa would live with her grandmother. Theresa did not like her grandmother, but given living with her mother like this and her grandmother, Theresa wished for her grandmother.

Theresa was an emotional wreck from this past year. Now her mother relocated her to the far Northwood. She had no friends here, no family, nothing of her own. She felt like a fish out of water. Her mother believed that by moving them out in the middle of nowhere her mother would be forced to stay sober. With no one to get high with and party, her mother would be okay. It was only under this condition that Theresa even consented to move out here. Theresa knew that her mother could not be alone, so here she was in the middle of nowhere away from everyone she knew.

Theresa Rowe hesitated outside Casey Baker's classroom. The other students talked about Mrs. Baker's class and said she was really tough on students, but they all seemed to like her. From the conversation, she figured Mrs. Baker to be a tough drill sergeant of types. So far, this school had done little to make her feel welcome or wanted. Theresa wondered if some of the talk about Mrs. Baker was for her benefit, to scare her as a joke. Theresa really was starting to hate this new school.

Taking a deep breath she walked into the classroom. Mrs. Baker was standing by the doorway greeting every student that entered. She was a small woman a little over five feet and weighing maybe one hundred pounds. *How could this woman be the same one the students talked about?* With a hand extended, "Hi, you must be my new student, Theresa. I'm Mrs. Baker, and I have a ton of paperwork for you and I will go over it with you in a minute once I get the rest of the class started." Casey reached out and shook Theresa's hand and turned her attention to the rest of the class.

Once the class was working, Casey approached Theresa and gave her "new student spiel."

"First, you need to understand that I do not work for the school. I work for a nonprofit in *partnership* with the school. What that means to *you* is that my class is not like any other class. If you work hard and give your best work, you will get an A and high school credit. If you do not work in this class, you're out. You fail and get zero credit. This paperwork has a contract that if you want to be in this class, you will sign, your parents or guardian will sign, and I will sign. I have emergency forms and blanket permission slips for you to fill out because right now we go off campus once a week and do community service, but we may go off campus for any other service work project that come up during the school year. I have a couple of "survey type" forms in there, too. The surveys are for me so I can know you better and help you the best way that I can. If you don't want to answer a question that is up to you, but tell me you don't want to answer it, so I don't think you did not understand the question. I have a reason for all the questions I ask and they are for my eyes alone. I promise you no one else will see them. If you take my class, what's in for you? I guarantee that you will be better prepared for life after high school, financial literacy skills, real world work experiences, and networking skills to name a few. You get an easy A because all you have to do is try, and you get high school credit towards graduation. I have a perfect record so far of my students transitioning to positive outcomes, meaning that every one of my students have graduated from high school and done something productive afterwards like college, work, trade school, military, etc. and I intend to keep my perfect record. I treat this class as a job because right now your job is to be a student. I believe that if you are going to do a job then you should do the best job you can. I promise to be completely honest with you meaning that if you are messing up I am going to tell you. I will tell you what I see, how to improve it, and I will work with you on how to do a better job. I will also tell you when you have done well and why. I don't believe that practice makes perfect, but I do believe in improving yourself every chance you get. I know this is a lot to take in so think it over, talk to other students, talk to your folks, siblings, pets and make a decision about whether you want to be in my class or not. Bottom line is, if you want to be in my class then I want you in my class. If you do not want to be in my class, then I don't want you here. I know that sounds harsh, but that is how I run this class."

The bell rings as Mrs. Baker finishes her monolog. Theresa looks around and the class is still sitting in their seats. Every other class the student almost sprinted out the door when the bell rand. Mrs. Bakers looks around the class.

"You may go. Have a great rest of the day." Casey addresses the whole class.

The students all get up to leave at the same time. Unbelievable, the whole class was waiting for the teacher to dismiss them. Theresa never saw anything like that. I guess that it is true that Mrs. Baker means business.

Theresa gathers up her paperwork. Casey smiles and asks, "So what do you think? Are you in?"

"I'm in." Theresa smiles and leaves the room.

"See you tomorrow." Casey calls out after her.

CHAPTER SEVEN

Theresa walks home and into the back door. She could hear her mother with a few "new" friends getting high in the living room. *Nothing ever changes. Promises made, promise broken.* Theresa and her mother, Rusty Rowe, were evicted after a drug raid on their apartment. Once upon a time Theresa had been a good student. Once upon a time Theresa wanted to earn a scholarship and go to college. Once upon a time Theresa had a baby sister. Today it was enough just to survive and make it through another day. Theresa was so angry all the time, her mother was at the center of her anger and blame.

"Terry is that you?" Her mother called out.

Terry, I hate that name. I think she does it on purpose to get me mad. Theresa did not respond to her mother, she just headed up the back steps to her bedroom. She knew her mother would never follow her up all those stairs.

Theresa flopped down on the old mattress and tried to go to sleep, anything to escape the scene going on downstairs. After a few minutes, Theresa knew that sleep would not come. She dug her homework out of her backpack and stared at the paperwork for Mrs. Baker. She wanted to be in Mrs. Baker's class, she had liked Mrs. Baker almost immediately. She made Theresa feel safe from the moment she entered the classroom. She was just this wisp of a woman and yet Theresa could sense there was a mother tiger in there. Just acknowledging my presence and not leaving me hanging was really appreciated. The other teachers made me feel stupid. *I like how she said that if I wanted to be there she wanted me there and if not, get out. I have never heard a teacher talk like that.*

Theresa signed her mother's name, Rusty Rowe, without bothering to ask even if her mother would sign. The less my mother is involved, the better off I am. Rusty Rowe had a way of destroying everything she touched. The reverse Midas touch instead of everything turning to gold, her mother turned everything to shit.

Theresa thought about that last night with her sister. None of this would have happened if mom could just stay sober. I know she didn't do this, but she is to blame. Tears steamed down her cheeks as she thought of her baby sister. Where are you? Did that monster really kill you like mom claims or did someone take you. Theresa was sure she would know if her sister was dead, but she truly believed that Alyssa was alive and needed her. *Damn you Mom, this is all your fault!* Shaking her head back and forth as tears streamed down her cheeks in total frustration. Theresa could not do anything. She could not help her mother, help her sister, or help herself for that matter. She realized what a truly useless person she was in this world.

TWO YEARS EARLIER

CHAPTER EIGHT

F BI Agent Timothy "Tim" Thibodeau approached the single family home noting the yellow crime tape. There were two marked patrol cars parked out front and other cars up and down the street. A crowd of spectators was milling about at a respectful distance. Tim parked his car half a block down the street and just sat and surveyed the scene. Experience had taught Tim that you could learn a lot about the crime by just surveying the crime scene and paying attention to the details or the lack of details. The workers were here from the crime lab, easily identified by their navy jackets lettered in bright yellow FBI on the front and back, they walking around the side of the house to the back with cameras. Tim noted that only 3 crime lab workers were present, generally there were a lot more. The group of spectators talked amongst themselves watching crime lab people. Tim could hear the voices, but not the content of their words.

The Christmas holiday was two weeks away, and most houses were decorated in some fashion. This house was absent of all holiday decorations. Tim found this curious considering a two-year-old girl lives here. The snow was drifting down promising maybe an inch of new snow. If you squinted your eyes, the scene with the holiday lights and spectators could almost be a Norman Rockwell painting of holiday carolers.

The house was a simple cape cod with aluminum siding, in reasonable condition suggesting fairly routine maintenance.

The aluminum siding dated the house because these days you have vinyl siding. A concrete stoop with three steps up to the front door with a rusty iron rail with the remnants of black paint. On the right side of the house was a driveway leading to a detached garage and a rear entrance to the house on the driveway side with a similar concrete stoop as the front of the house. Two window wells on the side indicated a basement unknown if finished or not.

The Amber Alert was for the daughter of a resident here, a two-year-old girl who went missing in the middle of the night. Unsure if the toddler had wandered off on her own or was kidnaped. The Amber Alert and the suspicion that it might be a kidnapping automatically brought in the FBI. Tim worked out of the Bangor office and was the agent-on-call, lucky him.

The river was just two blocks away, and a team of divers from the Warden Services had already been called to start looking. So far there was little to go on, the girl's father was her biological father that had only recently been granted custody of the girl because the mother had been arrested for drugs and was currently in a rehabilitation center. The father lived her with his grandmother and the occasional girlfriend that spent the night. The father age twenty-eight worked full time at the paper mill and had been working there steady for the past year. Prior to his job at the paper mill, he had had a series of odd jobs working as a mechanic or as a cook at local restaurants. The father had his high school diploma and served six years in the Army. The missing girl was a result of a one-night stand with the mother. The father took financial responsibility from day one. There is little to suggest that he had much contact with his daughter prior to the state placing her with him only recently.

Tim had stalled long enough, taking in the scene, he got out of his government issued blue Ford, stretched, and headed for the front of the house. He cupped his hands in front of his mouth and breathed on them to keep his fingers warm. As he moved past the crowd of spectators, he held up his FBI credentials. The act of identifying himself was a formality considering his face was known to most of these men working the scene.

"What have we got?" Tim asked out loud to anyone listening as he walked into the house.

"John LeClair, State Police." Introducing himself with his hand outstretched.

"Special Agent Timothy Thibodeau, FBI Bangor Office." Tim shook his hand and repeated, "What have we got?"

"Not a whole lot. The father, Andy Morrell, said that his daughter was asleep in her bed last night at about ten when he checked on her and was missing this morning at eight when we went to look in. Warden Services have been called to search the woods and river. Apparently there were a few people over her last night, and we are tracking everyone down to get a statement. The grandmother, Denise Morrell, says that she was here and went to bed around eight last night. She stated was watching TV in her bed and fell asleep, not real sure of the exact time." John stated reading off his notes.

"Where is the girl's bedroom?" Tim asked.

"In the basement, I'll show you. Follow me." John began walking towards the kitchen and opened the door between the living room area and the kitchen. The lights to the basement were already turned on, and there were people down there taking pictures. The air felt damp and had a musty smell. The floor was concrete at the bottom of the stairs indicating that the basement was at least partially unfinished. At the bottom of the stairs to the right, there was sheet rock and a small living space with an old couch and chair and another room that had a door, presumably the bedroom. Tim entered the small bedroom and saw a single twin size bed, unmade, with blue patterned sheets and a sleeping bag for a blanket.

"I think we found blood." Called out of the lab technicians.

Tim turned his attention towards the voice. In the open living space, the technicians were crouched down by a chair looking at the carpet, Tim could not see what the lab technician was looking at from this distance. If it was blood, the amount was too small to be the cause of death. Tim let the technicians do their job and turned back towards the bedroom. The room had a smell of cleaning chemicals, but the damp dank smell of the basement permeated the space. *What a sad place to sleep* Tim thought. The room had a few toys, a nightstand with a lamp, sheetrock walls painted white and nothing on them. The technicians were just finishing spraying the room down with luminal, standard procedure in missing children cases. The luminal would react with the blood and glow in the dark.

The technician stepped back and turned off the lights. Tim gasps as the whole room glowed there was evidence of blood everywhere.

"Take everyone into custody, the father, the grandmother, anyone who was here last night. I'll meet them at the station house." Tim barked out orders breaking the stunned silence. *We are not looking for a missing child, we're looking for a missing body.*

CHAPTER NINE

Using a field kit, the lab technician reported evidence of minor drug use, trace of marijuana, and drinking in the living room, but no way to say exactly when in the past week. The spots in the living space in the basement did turn out to be blood, the blood type was consistent with the missing girl, but it still took time run a DNA test, it's not like the movies when they have results the next day. The little girl and father both had the same blood type, meaning that the blood could be the father's.

Depending on how backed up the lab was, the DNA tests could take up to two weeks.

Andy Morrell, the father, had no criminal background. He served in the military without distinction, nothing stellar, but no problems either. He was honorably discharged after his six years and had returned to Maine and moved in with his grandmother. He lived continually with his grandmother and had regular employment since his discharge from the Army. Nothing remarkable about him, his habits, or his lifestyle, and yet Tim liked him for being responsible for the disappearance of his daughter. The amount of blood spelled torture, passionate crime. Tim's sixth sense was telling him that Andy was directly involved in the brutal slaying of his two-year old daughter. Something about his demeanor was cold and heartless and it gave Tim the creeps. The only problem was proving it. At this point Tim had no idea of what really happened here last night and who else might have been involved.

Andy seemed to be responding to the interrogation honesty with no embellishment. Most people, regardless of guilt or innocents, tended to talk a lot in police stations, they would go on and on about nothing and everything. The key was to listen and read them. Andy seemed relaxed and had an answer for everything, but just simple responses. The problem with having an answer for everything is that in the real world people seldom have answers for why they do the things that they do, but this guy here, he did. There was no storytelling from Andy, he declined any offer of food or drink and just asked that they continue and get done so he could leave. Tim turned up the interrogation.

"Do you do illegal drugs?" Tim asked.

Andy shifted in his seat and said, "No."

"We found evidence of illegal drug use in your house."

"Not my house."

"Where is Alyssa?"

"I don't know."

"Did you hurt Alyssa?"

"No, she was my kid."

"How can you not know where she is?"

"I told you I put her to bed and when I got up this morning she was gone."

"Do you know of anyone hurting Alyssa?"

Andy shifted again, "No, I already told you she was fine when she went to bed. Do I need a lawyer?"

"I don't know, do you?" Tim asked staring him straight into the eyes. Just then, a knock at the door and the guard waved to Tim to step out. Tim opened the door and spoke to the officer. Turning back to Andy Tim said, "Your lawyer is here." Andy looked genuinely surprised.

"Jeff Petersen I am Mr. Morrell's attorney. Are you charging my client?"

"No charges yet." Tim stated.

"Then we are leaving." Jeff said and motioned for Andy

to stand and follow him. Andy got up hesitantly looking at the officer, but no one told him to sit back down. Andy walked over to the door with his attorney, and the two of them walked out of the interrogation room and out of the police station. Andy tried to speak with his attorney, but he shook his head and tilted it towards the door indicating to wait until they were both outside.

"Make your client available counselor." Tim called after the couple as they left the station. Jeff waved good-bye. *Shit! That was my best chance of getting anything out of him! Wally, Habermash, and Frederickson, how in the world can Andy Morrell afford such a high-powered law firm?*

CHAPTER TEN

J eff Petersen escorted Andy out of the station house without saying a word. Andy had tried to ask him a question, but Mr. Petersen cut him off by shaking his head no, indicating not here.

Once outside, Jeff pointed to a black shiny sedan, "That's me. Get in."

"I have my truck right over there." Andy indicates by pointing towards the police parking lot.

"I'll bring you back, just get in so we can drive and talk."

Andy got into the car. Soft black leather, "Nice car."

"Thanks."

They drove away together and returned about twenty minutes later. Tim was just getting ready to leave when he saw the lawyer's car return. Andy exited his attorney's Audi A8 with Massachusetts's plates without looking back. He slammed the car door and rushed over to his truck. He looked scared. Tim watched the scene play out from the front steps of the station house. Tim wondered what that was all about, maybe Andy's lawyer told him what this was going to cost.

Andy hopped into his truck and took off immediately heading in the direction of his grandmother's house. The black sedan stayed at the curb until Andy's truck was out of sight. Tim could not tell if the lawyer was waiting for Andy to leave or if the Attorney was simply on the phone. The black sedan with Massachusetts's plates did a U-turn and headed in the opposite direction. *That was strange, but interesting,* Thought Tim.

CHAPTER ELEVEN

Andy knew the men he was dealing with were dangerous. He just did not know how well connected they were. He was surprised by the speed they were able to get him out of police custody. The lawyer told him that it was unlikely any charges would ever be filed, there was no evidence as long as Andy kept his mouth shut. Getting him that lawyer, from that law firm, that fast to the police station just to shut him up, demonstrated serious connections and for the first time Andy was scared, really scared. Andy Morrell was in way over his head playing games with big boys that did not play by any rulebook. Andy realized that he had made a deal with the devil and for what a couple of bucks? Andy was beginning to understand the gravity of his mistake, but it was too late to take it back now.

Andy was haunted by what the lawyer told him. *"We're keeping you alive only because killing you would raise suspicion, but if you so much as hint to the truth, we will do what we need to do and no one and I mean no one will find your body."* The lawyer's words played over and over in his head as he drove home.

Andy pulled into the driveway right up to the garage door. He parked so close to the garage door that there was no room to pass in front of the truck and the garage door. Andy sat there a few moments collecting his thoughts before going inside. Andy had never known fear like this, three tours of duty in Iraq was a picnic compared to this.

"What have you done?" His grandmother pounced the moment Andy walked into the house. Andy had barely entered the backdoor the opened up into the kitchen before his grandmother was questioning him. Andy's grandmother knew that whatever was happening, her grandson was behind it. "WHAT HAVE YOU DONE?" She shouted at him.

"Nothing, I swear." Andy held up his arms in a surrender fashion. "You know I would never harm anyone, especially my own flesh and blood. Alyssa was here and then she was gone. That's it. I didn't *do* ANYTHING TO HER!" Andy was shouting as he finished. His lie fell flat and convinced no one. Now his grandmother was convinced that Andy had done something to Alyssa.

His grandmother sat there studying her grandson's face. She had known him his whole life. He was a skillful liar. She wanted to believe him. It was too awful to think otherwise. Did she raise a monster? She sat still for a long time trying to read her grandson. He's lying, she could almost taste the bitter bile in her throat. When Andy dug in like this, she knew he would never back down and change his story. If she kept pushing him, she would never learn the truth and that sweet baby girl. The grandmother shuddered thinking of what could possible have happened to her sweet great-granddaughter. Trying to placate him and to let him think she believed him, his grandmother softened her tone and patted his arm. "Well, let's hope they find her soon." She sighed and left the room.

They are never going to find her.

CHAPTER TWELVE

Jeff watched Andy half walk half jog back to his truck. Jeff was wondering when his job at attorney had turned into enforcer for the mob. He was a hell of a litigator and he had done very well at the firm, made partner by the age of thirty. Andy Morrell was a two-bit nothing and Jeff was put out having to talk to someone of his level. After all, Jeff was a senior partner in one of the most prestigious law firms in the state, hell on the East Coast. Just riding in the same car with Andy made Jeff feel dirty.

Jeff reached into the glove box of his car and pulled out a small throw away phone. He dialed a number for memory. "Problem handled, he knows what he needs to do and what will happen if he doesn't"

The person on the other end of the line only listened and hung up.

Jeff dialed another number by memory. "Let's keep our eyes on our friend and make sure he knows he is being watched."

"Will do." The voice on the other end of the phone was all business, no emotion, and terrifying. Two simple words and they sent a tingle up Jeff's back.

Jeff started his car and drove away making sure he followed all the traffic rules. He was in no mood to be pulled over just now. As he approached the bridge over the Kennebec River, he rolled the passenger side of the window down. When he reached the middle of the bridge, he threw the phone off the bridge into the river. The move was effortless with the air of having done this move many times before. In fact, Jeff was quite skilled at destroying evidence. As a litigator, he was top notched, but thinking like a criminal he was even better.

Jeff drove the hour to his ocean front estate in Kennebec. The thought of standing on his terrace looking out at the crashing waves was calming. Thinking about the girl, mother a drug addict and dad a no good two-bit punk, the girl was better off no matter where she ended up. Watching the news reports, the kid was a cute kid, but what kind of future did she have? She would have been bounced between mom and dad in between drug treatments, relapses, and god knows what else.

There was no doubt that Jeff was a good guy anymore, but in this particular case he was feeling that maybe a little bit of what was good and decent was still there. In this case, Jeff was on the right side even if it was the wrong side of the law. Taking comfort in those thoughts, Jeff was pleased to think that maybe what he did wasn't all bad.

CHAPTER THIRTEEN

Tim commandeered the main conference room for the investigation's central command of the Alyssa Rowe case. Tim grimace thinking about Jeff Peterson walking into the interrogation room and out with the only real viable suspect. The girl's father lawyering up like that with such a high profile lawyer was quite a wrinkle. The amount of blood was indicative of serious trauma. The blood indicated substantial injury and blood loss. Tim was fairly sure that he was looking at a murder and not a kidnapping. Thinking back to lectures on violent crimes against children Tim recalls the fact that in cases of children the perpetrator is almost always family. *Fact: Ninety percent of all violent acts against children are committed by someone known to the child.* That statistic kept running through Tim's mind as he sorted through the facts in the case. Thinking about the idea that violent crime against children is by family, Tim reviewed the case again. The only family members present or who had access to Alyssa were the grandmother and the dad.

Tim posted the crime scene photos on the white board along side of a picture of the two-year-old. Tim was recalling the moment the technician turned off the lights in Alyssa bedroom. That had been shocking, Tim had never seen anything so grisly before and it was a green glowing light it wasn't red like the scene in Carrie. What must it have been like to be there for the actual event? Surely no normal person could witness that and not have a lasting impression. There is so much blood. If Andy was involved and witnessed this, he was one cool customer to sit in custody and calmly answer the questions. So far, the lab had not reported back on the DNA.

On one wall was a satellite image of the crime scene with a ten-mile radius from the house marked off, the river was so close to the house. The distance from the house to the river is only minutes on foot. It would be so easy to dump Alyssa into the river. The river would carry the body downstream and before you know it, the body would be out to sea, long gone. The entry point into the river closest to the house presented few obstacles for the body to move downstream to the ocean. There were no dams or landforms that would obstruct the body. Tim knew this, but the question was, did Andy Morrell know this? Probably, living this close to the river it would be unlikely that Andy was not familiar with the river.

Andy murdered his daughter and dumped her in the river. Or at least he knows who did. I know it like I know own face. How does Jeff Petersen play into all of this. There is no way that Andy has the resources to hire him or to even have a chance meeting with him. Someone else is involved that is the only way to explain Jeff Petersen. Tim had a really bad habit of going with gut, like a dog with a bone. His gut feelings had a history of working to Tim's advantage, but he was a cop and he needed to follow the evidence not his gut. Right now the evidence was pointing right at the biological father, Andy Morrell.

CHAPTER FOURTEEN

What a dump! The man sat in an older work van with Collins Electric printed on the side. He parked just two doors down from Andy Morrell's home. He knew his van would stick out like a sore thumb because neighborhood like these know everything and everyone on the block and his van did not belong there. He was under instructions to make his presence and surveillance known, but not obvious. The money was good and that is all he ever cared about. He liked his job. He would get a call with instructions without ever meeting face to face. No one knew who he was and if anything went wrong there was no one to blame. Even the guy who called him tonight knew who he was. *I work in the shadows, I live in the shadows, and that's how I like it.*

Just past midnight the bedroom light goes on and within five minutes my target is out the back door and backing up his truck. *He's on the run.* The man watches the truck backup braking at the street turn right on the street away from the man.

As the taillights fade down the roadway, the man starts the van and pursues with his lights off. A clear night and full moon make pursuit without lights easy. *Andy what are you doing? You can't run from me!* Andy takes the southbound ramp on I-95 and merges into traffic without noticing the van following him. Andy heads south on I-95 for a while traveling just under seventy-five miles per hour. *He knows the ten-mile over rule, cops pull you over at ten miles over the speed limit, but not nine.* Andy takes the Waterville exit and heads east. *Where are we going?* He watches Andy pull into a gas station and pull up to the pump. *He didn't plan this he did not have a full tank of gas. He's using his credit card. Amateur.* The man places a call. "He's on the run, what do you want me to do?"

CHAPTER FIFTEEN

T he low fuel light illuminates on Andy's dash. *Damn!* Andy knows that he can drive another forty miles after the light comes on, but forty miles is not far enough. He takes the next exit and pulls into a gas station.

Andy pulls up to the pump and gets out of the truck. He opens the cover on his gas tank and puts the gas cap on the rail of his truck bed. He swipes his debit card, presses the lowest grade gas selection, raises the handle, and starts pumping. Completely unaware of the driver sitting in a green electrical van making a phone call. At that moment, a computer terminal pinged with Andy's exact location.

For the first time in weeks, Andy felt free. *I'll just go away, and no one will ever find me.* The phone in Andy's pocket started vibrating. Andy pulls the phone out and sees the caller ID. A sick penetrating dread fills his body, Andy knows the number. He's trapped he wants desperately to throw the phone as far from him as he can, but he knows better than to ignore it.

Holding the receiver to his ear Andy heard the voice say, "I know where you are, and I know what you are thinking. There is nowhere on earth that you can hide where I cannot find you. Finish filling up your tank and go home." Click. The line goes dead.

Andy's knees buckled beneath him, and Andy fell to the ground hitting his head on the curb of the gas pump. Click. The truck was full of gas, but Andy knew there was only one place he could go. *Home.*

CHAPTER SIXTEEN

Sitting around the conference table of Alyssa Rowe command central, the investigators reviewed the facts of the case.

"What do we know about the dad and grandmother?" Tim asked standing at the whiteboard marker in hand.

"Dad, Andy Morrell did a few years in the Army after high school, honorably discharged without distinction. Worked odd jobs in restaurants and finally landed his laborer job at the paper mill. No criminal record as adult or juvenile. Met our Vic's (short for victim) mother at a bar the Vic is the result of an apparent one nightstand. Served papers by the Department of Human Social Services naming him the biological father and subsequent court order for child support. He paid all his child support every month on time through the court leaving a record of current support payments. He has a high school diploma nothing remarkable, never violent, no trouble whatsoever. His current girlfriend, on the other hand, is a piece of work. This girl is all trouble. Karen Tanneger, age 28, sister to El Guapo out of Miami heavily involved in the Miami drug scene. Karen has a long history of arrests for drug trafficking, prostitution, battery and assault, and it goes on. Thing is that Karen has never seen the inside of a courtroom. Lots of charges, but nothing ever sticks, like she is made of Teflon. Her attorney is top notch and has been able to get all charges dismissed without prejudice for one reason or another. Wanna guess who her attorney is?"

Officer Carlson raised his eyebrows.

"Don't tell me, Jeff Petersen from the law offices of Wally, Habermash, and Frederickson." Tim stated incredulously. *No such thing as coincidences.*

"You got it." Chimed Officer Carlson. *And* it explains Jeff's appearance at the station house helping Andy. Officer Carlson continues rundown of the father and grandmother, "Grandmother, Denise Morrell, age 68 retired from the paper mill in town. Same paper mill her grandson works at. Husband George Morrell died over twenty years ago in a hunting accident. Has lived at the current address for the past forty plus years. Andy is Denise's son's kid. Denise's son, George Jr., shot himself within days of his dad's accident in the family home. He had sole custody of Andy because the mother did not want him and gave him up at birth. Far as we know, Andy's mother has never had any contact with her son and we don't know if Andy knows who she is. With George Jr. dead, Denise is granted the sole guardian of Andy. No criminal activity here with the Grandmother. I think we should focus on the girlfriend and whoever was there that night." Officer Carlson finished up.

"Agree, but both Andy and the girlfriend are lawyered up, so we need to figure out a way around them. Find out who was there and see if we can get them in here." Tim stared at the whiteboard that now added Andy Morrell and Karen Tanneger under the suspect column. The conference room phone rang in the background and Tim could hear the pick up, pause, and then asking the called to hang on.

"Tim, the lab is on the line." Said Sam one of the task force members.

"Put it on speaker." Tim directed

"The blood spots found are consistent for Alyssa. The rest of the blood found in the basement is not human." The lab technician reported.

"What kind of blood is it?" Tim asked unable to hide his surprise.

"Best guess, its blood from butchering a deer or moose. I'll send a full report to your office, but thought you would want to know this right away" The lab technician stated.

Andy's grandfather was a hunter and possibly his dad, I wonder if Andy is a hunter too? Tim thought. "Thanks for the information" Tim said his good-byes and nodded to Sam to disconnect the call.

"So what does this mean? Is Alyssa alive? Is there hope?" Tim said out loud to no one in particular.

CHAPTER SEVENTEEN

Theresa prided herself at being a top student. She enjoyed learning and academics just made sense to her. Her mother's drug addiction and lifestyle, often interfered with school and studying. Being the child of a drug addict had its own challenges that often went unnoticed by everyone else. Theresa mused at the difficulties of explaining that she was tired because her mother was partying all night. Her mother's on again off again drug use was the story of Theresa's life. Theresa's mother was high on drugs when Theresa was conceived. Theresa never knew her birth father and her mother claimed to not know either. Her baby sister was a result of mom getting high and having a one nightstand with some guy up near Newport. That guy was good about paying child support, but never came to visit with her. Theresa little sister represented everything good in Theresa's life. Despite the fact that her mother could not remain sober for the duration of the pregnancy and her prenatal care was sketchy, the result was a perfect little sister. Theresa worried that there would be long lasting permanent damage to her sister, but so far she was the cutest little two-year-old ever. Her science report was due at the end of the week and was a major part of this semester's grade. Her mother's addiction had one silver lining, it motivated Theresa to work hard and hope for a scholarship to college. School was Theresa's way out and when Theresa got out she was taking her little sister with her.

The librarian came over to tell Theresa it was time to close up. Theresa was almost finish with her assignment, and could easily finish it in the morning. Theresa packed up her backpack and started the walk home. It was a chilly night, but clear. *Mom should be passed out by now. I hope Alyssa is fed and in her crib.*

The moment Theresa rounded the corner to her home she saw the emergency lights. There were two squad cars and an ambulance. Theresa immediately started running for the house. She saw them carrying out her mother on a stretcher. As Theresa got close enough to touch her mother someone grabbed her up and pulled her away.

"Stop! That's my mom!" Theresa shouted and thrashed at the unknown person keeping her from her mother.

"Your mom is going to the hospital and we taking the baby into protective custody. Do you have someone we can call to come get you?" A woman explained to her as Theresa began to take everything in and stopped struggling against the person holding her back.

Theresa stared at the woman and slowly realized that she was from social services, and they were taking Alyssa away. "No wait, Alyssa can come with me to our grandmother's house." Theresa explained.

"No, you can go to your grandmother's house, but Alyssa has to come with us for now, it's a matter of policy." The woman stated matter-of-factly.

They loaded her mother into the ambulance and slowly pulled away from the curb.

"What's going to happen to her?" Theresa asked.

"They will take her to the hospital for an evaluation and then go from there. Most likely the recommendation will be a treatment facility for drugs and alcohol, but that will be up to the Judge. This incident is likely to violate her probation."

"When can I see her and my sister?"

"Soon, I don't know when."

Theresa was frustrated by the lack of definitive answers. Her mother was gone, for how long was anyone's guess. Her sister was gone to protective services and where she was placed was anyone's guess.

"Alyssa has a father in the Waterville area." Theresa yelled out to the lady.

"Thanks, we'll take that into consideration." The lady responded half-heartedly.

Theresa sat on the front stoop and called her grandma. "Grandma, can you come get me? They've taken momma and sissy away."

"I'll be right there." Theresa's grandmother said and hung up.

CHAPTER EIGHTEEN

Theresa was standing in the shadows outside of Andy Morrell's house watching her baby sister playing. The lady from social services must have listen to Theresa and placed Alyssa with Andy, the biological dad. Alyssa had a cast on her left arm. *When did she break her arm?* Theresa wandered. *Is this why the police were called to her house in the first place?* Theresa had not spoken to her mother since the night they took her away. The judge violated her probation and sent her to a drug rehabilitation facility out of state. Whether or not Theresa's mother would have jail time when she returned was still up in the air, a lot depended on how cooperative she was in rehab. Theresa was unclear as to why and how the police became involved this time, but seeing Alyssa's arm she wondered if her mother on one of her mother's many boyfriends hurt Alyssa. *I should have brought to the library with me. I never should have left her alone with mom.*

Theresa was watching her sister's new family play with her. There was a man and old lady. Theresa assumed the man was Alyssa's dad and she was unsure who the old lady was, but probably a family member. Theresa liked the way the old lady and Alyssa's dad were playing with her sister. Theresa watched the three eat dinner and then move to the living room to play games and watch TV. Theresa could not bear to tear herself away from watching her sister. The judge had given her mother a choice of six months in a rehabilitation center or one year in jail.

Her mother chose the rehabilitation center. Theresa was living with her grandmother, her mother's mother, but it wasn't going so well. Every day her grandmother complained about Theresa's mom. Every sentence would begin with "your mom this or your mom that." Theresa found it interesting that her grandmother never started her sentences with "my daughter this or that" as if the problems were all Theresa's doing and she had no responsibility at all in how her daughter turned out. Theresa wanted to scream at her to stop dumping on her mother, but she was too scared to say anything.

It looked like they were all going to bed, and Theresa made the decision to sneak into the house and visit with her sister. She watched Andy take Alyssa down to the basement and retire himself to the upstairs. The old woman disappeared to the back of the house presumably her bedroom.

Theresa waited another half hour for good measure when she crept into the house. The backdoor entered into the kitchen. The backdoor was unlocked, no one in Maine bothered locks their doors and probably did not know where the keys were. People from away found this to be quaint, but Theresa knew better. There was nothing folksy or quaint about keeping door unlocked, Mainers were as a whole lazy and did not want to be bothered carrying around keys, same reason that they almost always left their keys in their vehicles.

The house was old and creaky, so Theresa had to move as slow and steady as possible. She reached the top of the basement stairs and paused listening to sounds. She could hear the TV from the back of the house. *Probably the old woman had a TV in her bedroom.* Theresa descended to the basement and saw mostly an unfinished basement. The place smelled musty and dank. There was some carpet down for a makeshift living room and some drywall up for rooms and storage. *This is where they are keeping my sister.* Theresa's thinking of her sister's care changed instantly. She found her sisters bedroom and entered. Her baby sister was already asleep, but Theresa felt better just being so near. Theresa heard footsteps on the basement steps, so she moved to the closet and hid.

CHAPTER NINETEEN

Theresa's heart raced, and the thumping was so loud. Crouched down at the back of the closet with her back against the wall, trying hard not to move. The floor of the closet was littered with boxes, clothing, and stuff. Every move that she made was so loud.

"We are talking about a hundred thousand dollars, cash. Not bad for a day's work. I mean it's not like she is really your kid, I mean she is, but she isn't. It's not like you really know the kid." Said a male voice.

"It's not the kid I care about. I don't want to get caught. I have never been to jail, and I want to keep it that way." Said a different male voice.

The two men were standing right in front of the closet. Theresa tried to hold her breath, but she had to breathe. Theresa could feel the heat of fear rising up her body. She was sure that if she looked at herself in the mirror she would look like a frightened deer in headlights. *What are they talking about? Are they talking about Alyssa? Are they going to do something to her? Why are they in Alyssa's room?*

Theresa's legs were cramping from crouching, but she was too scared to move. Trickles of sweat rolled down her forehead and threaten to roll into her eyes. Too scared to wipe her brow, her breathing became rapid and shallow, Theresa again tried to hold her breath squeeze her eyes shut and began counting in her head. Theresa was on number three hundred eighty-five when she realized the men had left the room.

She peeked out of the closet through the crack in the door jam causing her to shift a weight a bit. This minor movement sent a sharp pain up her legs followed by the sensation of pins and needles. Her legs had falling asleep. She massaged her legs and the pain subsided a bit, but was still there.

Theresa pushed the closet door open about an inch and waited for some kind of reaction. Nothing. She pushed the door open a few more inches. Nothing. As quietly as possible she crept out of the closet until she was standing in front of her sister's crib. Alyssa was sound asleep.

"Alyssa" she whispered.

Nothing. Alyssa kept sleeping. *She has never been that deep of a sleeper.* Theresa reached her hand into the crib and shook Alyssa. "Wake up sweetheart, sissy is here." Nothing.

Theresa could hear footsteps walking about upstairs. Quietly Theresa climbed the basement stairs to the kitchen. The door to the kitchen was open, Theresa could hear the TV playing in the living room and muffled voices. The backdoor was about fifteen feet from the basement door. Theresa scuttles across the kitchen floor, eases the backdoor open and slips outside. Gently Theresa closed the door to the house and retreated walking backwards into the neighbor's yard. Theresa moved behind the shrubs around the neighbor's house and watched the house. No one was following her. Theresa hightails it back to her grandmother's house with no idea what to do next.

CHAPTER TWENTY

The sun was just coming up when Theresa heard her grandmother moving about in the kitchen. After sneaking into the house and up to her room, Theresa tried to sleep, but she just lay there thinking about her little sister. She tried to make sense from the conversation she overhead in her sister's room. From her hiding spot in the closet, Theresa was unable to see the men talking, but she assumed one of the men talking had been Andy, Alyssa's dad. Theresa had a bad feeling about this and the thought made her queasy. Theresa was at a loss what to do next. How could she explain what she overheard, how she came to be in that house, hiding in the closet. The fact that Alyssa did not wake when she tried to rouse her, bothered Theresa. *Something is wrong. Something is very wrong.*

Theresa got out of bed and made her way downstairs before he grandmother could yell at her to wake up. Her grandmother was sitting at the kitchen table with her coffee smoking a cigarette looking much older than she was.

"Those things will kill you," Theresa quipped.

"Speak for yourself, gallivanting about all hours of the night. I will not stand for another one of you running about doing drugs and getting pregnant."

Theresa flushed red from the remark, but unable to tell the truth about last night she chose to remain mute. *If only you really knew what was going on you old bat.* Grabbing an apple and her backpack Theresa headed out the back door to school. It was way too early, but she did not want to stay a minute more with her grandmother's condemnation.

Her grandmother called after her, "Come home right after school we are going to see that worthless mother of yours and I don't like driving in the dark!"

Theresa waved acknowledgment, but did not turn around to face her grandmother she did not want her to see the tears streaming down her face. *Thanks, grandma, I love you too!*

CHAPTER TWENTY-ONE

John LeClair from the State Police stood at the podium looking out at the crowd. "At this point we are still hopeful that Alyssa Rowe is still alive. We have the Warden Service and numerous volunteers searching the woods and riverbanks for any sign of her. An Amber alert went out over the wire within minutes of the report of her missing. We are following several leads, but so far nothing has turned up."

"Do you suspect foul play?" A reporter from Channel 5 yelled out.

"We are exploring a multitude of scenarios. What we know is that Alyssa Rowe was at home in her bed at 10 pm Wednesday and sometime in the night she went missing. The 911 call reporting her missing was made just after eight thirty in the morning on Thursday.

"What about the Dad? Is it true that he was brought in for questioning?" The reporter asked.

"Yes, strictly routine. We are questioning everyone who was in the home that evening. Our prayers are with the family, and we ask that anyone who has information on the whereabouts of Alyssa Rowe to contact the police as soon as possible. That is all we have at this time. Thank you and good night." John LeClair turned away from the press and hurried into the building.

John had been told, in no uncertain terms, that this was a missing person's case. So far there was no physical evidence to support foul play and as much as he personally liked the father for this he had nothing, not a shred of evidence to connect the father with his missing daughter. As far as John was concern, the problem with treating this case as a missing person instead of a murder investigation was the allocation of resources and personnel. At this point, John's investigation was limited to search and rescue. His fear that valuable evidence was being overlooked or corrupted by not properly processing the scene as a murder scene, went unanswered. Andy and Denise Rowe were back in the house doing God knows what to any evidence left behind. John had half a mind to ignore the directive and continue this as a murder investigation, but his job was on the line. This was an election year and the powers to be were serious in their orders. John wondered how politically savvy it was to ignore a potential child murderer and deny adequate support to properly investigate?

CHAPTER TWENTY-TWO

Tim watched the press conference and was confused. *What is going on?* We already went to the judge and got an arrest warrant for Andy Morrell. The blood drops on the rug in combination with the broken arm demonstrated a presumption of foul play. Waiting only allowed for the potential of contamination of the crime scene. Right now Andy and his mother were living in the house and Tim could think of a million things Andy might be doing to get rid of evidence. Tim was concerned that they had no body, but they had prosecuted murder cases without a body in the past.

The phone rang, and Tim answered it on the second ring. "Agent Timothy Thibodeau" The caller was from the regional office in Boston.

"Hi Agent Thibodeau, I'm Mike Rand Assistant Deputy Director"

An awkward pause as Tim swallowed a lump in his throat, "Deputy Director, what can I do for you?"

"You need to stand down in terms of proceeding with your arrest on Andy Morrell." Mike Rand's voice was calm and smooth.

"I don't understand." Tim questioned.

"This is a missing child and nothing more. There is

insufficient evidence to suggest otherwise."

"But what do you mean we don't have sufficient evidence?"

"We have reasons to believe that Alyssa is alive and that Andy Morrell had nothing to do with his daughter's disappearance"

"May I inquire to the nature of your information?"

"I am not at liberty to say and it is above your pay grade." Mike's voice was tinged with irritation.

Tim listened to the other end of the phone and was told to "call off the dogs," so to speak, no one was going to arrest Andy Morrell not now or not ever. Tim was sputtering protests, when he was told his job was on the line, and the phone went dead.

"Son of a Bitch!" Tim threw the phone against the wall leaving a two-inch hole in the wall. "What the hell just happen?" His cell phone vibrated on the conference table. "What?"

"Are you investigating Alyssa Rowe?" A young female voice said on the phone.

"Yes."

"Alyssa Rowe is alive. Her father, Andy Morrell, did something with her, I don't know what. I'm scared for her. Please help her. " The phone disconnected.

Tim just stared into the dead phone. *This is the second person to tell me that Alyssa Rowe is alive in just a matter of minutes.* Wondering what to do with this, Tim copied the phone number on the caller ID and stared at the number. Could be another crazy, get a case like this and the crazies come out of the woodwork. Tim might just leave it at that, but the Assistant Deputy Director had said pretty much the same thing only that Andy Morrell was not involved.

CHAPTER TWENTY-THREE

Theresa hung up the phone and immediately felt the weight of the world off her shoulders. Now they would find her sister and arrest that jerkoff of a father. None of this would have happened if mom had stayed sober. Then again, we never would have had Alyssa if mom had stayed sober. *I should have taken her with me when I was there. She was right there sleeping and I knew they were planning something, but what do I do I just run away and leave her there. I can blame mom all I want, but I'm the one who left her there knowing.*

Grandmother had been fairly decent since Alyssa went missing, almost nice. Theresa thought she heard her grandmother crying one night, but when she went down to check her grandmother growled for her to go away calling her a nosey spy.

"Hey, grandmother what do you want for dinner?"

"I'm not hungry. You fix something for yourself." Grandmother called from her room.

Theresa walked to her grandmother's bedroom doorway and looked in. Her grandmother was still in her bathrobe. It was clear that her grandmother had not changed her clothes all day. She unkempt and did not seemed to have showered either. This was not like her grandmother, usually up with the sun ready to go. The TV on her dresser was turned on, and her grandmother was lying down in bed.

Knocking on the door jam Theresa asks, "Are you feeling alright?"

"I'm fine. I just don't feel like eating."

"You have to eat something. How about I make you some soup and toast?"

"For the love of God, I said I wasn't hungry why do you all have to make such a big deal out of everything?"

"Sorry, I was just trying to help." Theresa turns to walk away and turns back towards her grandmother. "She's going to be alright, she's going to come home. I know it."

"Who are you talking about?"

"Alyssa, I just know it."

"Don't talk about things you know nothing about. Just go, leave me be." Her grandmother snarled.

Theresa turned around and went to the kitchen. She made a grilled cheese and tomato soup for dinner. For the first time since her mother was taken away she felt happy. *It's all going to work out, you'll see.*

CHAPTER TWENTY-FOUR

Nothing worked out as Theresa had hoped. She really believed that her one phone call would blow the whole case wide open, but nothing came of it. She expected that the agent would call her back with questions, but he never called. The search for Alyssa has gone cold. No one ever mentions her anymore. No happy reunions with the family as Theresa had imagined. Six months past and Denise Rowe returned home, clean and sober. With no place to stay, Denise moved in with her mother and Theresa.

The first thing Rusty Rowe does when she gets home is to call a press conference suggesting she has new information about her daughter's disappearance. Theresa asked her about this new information, but all her mom would tell her is that she would have to wait like everyone else. When the day came for the press conference, Rusty used the opportunity to grandstand and accuse the police of sloppy investigation. She demanded that Andy Morrell be arrested and tried for killing her precious daughter. Theresa was outraged that her mother would take this opportunity to make this all about her.

The search for Alyssa stalled completely and the assumption was that Andy Morrell killed and dumped the body in the river. Special Agent Tim Thibodeau was unable to proceed with a murder conviction and was told that unless he had a body the assumption was missing persons. The political pressure brought to bear in this case was unlike anything Tim had known. It did not help matters that Rusty Rowe, Alyssa's mother, found every opportunity to tell the press that the police were incompetent and demand that Andy Morrell be arrested for her daughter's disappearance. Tim would think that the politics of a grieving mother would allow for him to reopen the investigation as a possible homicide, but even that did not seem to matter. Andy Morrell was not to be touched, he was being protected and Tim had no idea why.

Alyssa Rowe's disappearance was shoved to the back pages of the news. With no new information the press stopped reporting on it. Rusty could rally press interest on the anniversary date of her daughter's disappearance, but for the rest of the world Alyssa Rowe was forgotten. Theresa withdrew from the world she felt angry and trapped all the time. She blamed her mother for everything. Theresa would replay the night that her mother was taken into custody and they lost Alyssa. *If only she had never been taken from them.* Rusty Rowe found a cause with her daughter and attended rallies about missing children, but she continued to drink and follow the drug scene. Theresa was stuck living with her mother and hating her at the same time.

State Police Officer John LeClair resigned shortly after the investigation stalled. Some say that his resignation was because of the Alyssa Rowe as a result case, but no one really knows. The rumors said that John LeClair left law enforcement and became a guide up in northern Maine. Grandmother Rowe had a massive coronary during a fight with her daughter about Alyssa and died shortly afterwards. The Alyssa Rowe case impacted a few individuals profoundly, but at the end of the day Alyssa Rowe was just another missing child added to the list of many other missing children around the country.

PRESENT DAY

CHAPTER
TWENTY-FIVE

"You have not turned in a single assignment since you transferred here. How do you expect to pass?" Sally did not know what to do to get through to this student.

"Maybe I don't care if I pass." Theresa slouched in a chair with her shoulders resting on the back of the chair. Theresa had transferred in recently and was showing signs of maladjustment. Her records indicated she was a top student, but so far she showed nothing. She refused to participate in class or do any work. She was moody, sullen, and radiated hostility. The only class she seemed to show any interest in was Casey's Consumer Economics class.

"How's Mrs. Baker's class going?" Sally changed the subject hoping to get a reaction from Theresa.

"It's okay." Truth was Theresa really liked Mrs. Baker. Mrs. Baker was straightforward and funny. Theresa felt safe in her class.

"No fights?" Theresa did not respond. Sally continued, "You seem really angry? How's your mom?"

"They sold her." Theresa blurted staring directly at Sally.

"What are you saying? Who?"

"Just that. They sold my sister for money."

"You get that I have to report this. Who are they?"

"That father of hers, don't know if mom was in on it. Mom is too busy getting high all the time, but we seemed to have some extra money after it happen. I reported it at the time, thought it would be all taken care of. Nothing happened. I hope you report it. I hope they listen to you. I hope they arrest their ass. Then maybe I can get my sister back!" Theresa screamed and ran out of the office.

Sally stunned by the outburst she just sat there staring at the empty doorway. When she got up, Theresa was gone. Sally walked down the hall to peek around the corner. No Theresa, no one. Everyone was in class. Sally walked to her desk and called the office. "Can you find Theresa Rowe?"

"Do you want me to page her?"

"No, she got upset and ran out of my office. I just wanted to see if she is still in the building.. Is Kelly in her office?"

"Yep."

"Tell her I have a situation and am coming right down to speak with her." Sally hung up. If anyone could find a student, it was Marla. *Now what? Where did that come from? What in the world was she talking about? Obviously she was talking about her sister, but what did it mean? You'd have to be living under a rock not to know the story of Alyssa Rowe, two-year-old that vanishes without a trace.*

Theresa Rowe ran out of the office and into the girl's locker room. *Get a grip.* She splashed water on her face and dried it with paper towels. She took several deep breaths and returned to class as if nothing had happened. *Deny, Deny, Deny.* The deep breathing helped. She walked into her class, sat down and joined the rest of the class.

CHAPTER TWENTY-SIX

The meeting with Kelly went as expected. Don't do anything until we know for sure. There is no imminent threat of harm so this is not a reportable offense and frankly this girl, Theresa, is unstable. Sally reached for the phone by her computer to make a call. Who could she call? She hangs the phone up and thinks. Kelly told her to her to do nothing. *No she said to wait until we had reliable information.* The only one Sally could think of to call was her friend Tim. Tim and Sally grew up together, their moms were best friends. They had even dated in high school, but soon realized that they were more buddies than lovers. Sally went into education and Tim went into the FBI.

"Tim old buddy old pal." Sally sing song into the phone.

"You want something from me. Get to the point I am very busy." Tim attempted to sound annoyed.

"You're an FBI agent in Bangor, Maine. How busy can you be?"

"Hey did you call me for a favor or to insult me? Seriously, I really am working hard." Tim was now really annoyed. He was an FBI agent in Bangor, Maine to be close to his family and that included Sally.

"You mean hardly working." Sally laughs at her own joke.

"I take it back, that was mean. I love that you are an FBI agent in Maine. Keeps you close and I really do appreciate that." Sally cajoles.

"And how convenient for you. Okay, what do you need?'

"A sounding board. I want to hear your honest thoughts and suggestions. Remember the Alyssa Rowe case?"

Sally told him about the incident with Theresa Rowe. The case had been all over the news when it first happened and then it just kind of faded. Sally did not know that her good friend Tim had been involved in the case. Tim was the only FBI agent she knew and so whenever she needed help he was her first call. Over the years, students had confided in Sally about their home lives, but this was the first time a family was accused of human trafficking. Tim agreed to check into this and asked that Sally sit on this until he had answers.

CHAPTER TWENTY-SEVEN

Tim sat at his desk mulling over the story his friend Sally had told him. He stared at the four words he had written down on his legal pad "they sold my sister" Sally and I go way back, we grew up together. She is the first woman I ever loved, maybe the last one I ever will love. Sally did not feel that kind of love for me, but I know she loves me in her own way, honest and true. So I hide my romantic feelings for her and help her out any chance I get. Those words, *they sold my sister...* Those were the same words from that caller. I never did follow up on that call because I thought it was another nut case. That was after the press conference. That was when I was order to stand down on the arrest of Andy Morrell. That was when Andy Morrell's fairy godmother would make him untouchable. A man no one knew or cared about prior to his daughter's disappearance. A man who would instantaneously become so important he was not to be touched. After all this time, he was brought back to that fateful night when word came down that the bureau was not pursuing criminal charges in the Alyssa Rowe case. He remembers the call from the girl and now regretted not following up on it.

Sally said that her information came from the older sister. What is her name? Tammy? Looking down at his note pad he was surprised to see he had not written any details of the conversation on those four words. *They sold my sister.* Did the older sister know something? Andy got up and went to a file cabinet on the wall and pulled his copy of the Alyssa Rowe file, the official copy was down in cold case files. Actually, it was not considered an FBI case, no evidence of crossing state lines, no ransom request to consider kidnapping, nothing. That wasn't possible she had no contact with Andy, the house, or her sister once she flipping though the file, Andy finds what he is looking for, the older sister's name is Theresa. According to this, Theresa was placed with the maternal grandmother and Alyssa was placed with her biological father. What information could this kid possible have? She wasn't anywhere near? Looking at his notes he realizes that this must have been the girl that called with the tip so many years ago. I need to get up north and interview this girl and see what she knows.

Tim checked his calendar to see when he was free to make a trip to Rosewood. *Who was he kidding? He is an FBI agent in Bangor, Maine, how busy can my schedule be.* Sally was right. There is not a lot of business for an FBI field officer in Bangor, Maine. Good excuse to visit with Sally. He would make a trip up to see Sally this week and see what he could find out about the sibling.

Tim grabbed the phone and called the State Police in Augusta.

"Hi, this is Special Agent Thibodeau is Officer John LeClair available?"

"I'm sorry, I have no listing for a John LeClair."

"What happened to him? Where did he go?"

"I'm new here. I never met the guy. He was before my time. Can I direct you to someone else?"

"I'm calling about the Alyssa Rowe case. Who is in charge of that?"

"If you don't mind holding? I'll find out and connect you."

"I'll hold. Thank you." Tim was on hold for several minutes listening to the most mind numbing music. Tapping his fingers while he waited Tim tried to recall the last time he spoke with Officer LeClair.

"Hi, this is Officer Brett Jenkins how may I help you?" A voice interrupted Tim's recollecting.

Tim explained the role he played in the initial investigation and wanted to know what the current status of the investigation, as a curtsey and nothing more. Brett explained that he was newly assigned to the case, as in the past week. He admitted he was not up to speed on the case, but fortunately had the case file right on his desk. He mentioned that the FBI notes from and Agent Thibodeau indicated that there was insufficient evidence to think consider this case anything more than a missing person's case, official recommendation by the FBI to send this back to the local jurisdiction for investigation. *Wow, Tim had never noted that nor would he have.*

"Where is the case today?" Tim asked trying to hide in surprise at his supposed notes on the case.

"The search was called off over after an additional six months and the case has been cold ever since."

"What is the sense in the department?"

"I couldn't say. Like I said I just got assigned this case and a cold case it is. Kid probably wandered out of the house at night and fell into the river."

"Where is Andy Morrell these days?" Tim asked the question, but he already knew the answer. Tim never believed Andy to be innocent of Alyssa's disappearance and deep down was convinced that Andy had murdered his daughter and dumped her in the river.

"Nothing in the file about Andy Morrell other than a notation that he was exonerated of all suspicion."

"Who wrote that?"

"Special Agent Timothy Thibodeau."

Exonerated of all suspicion. Those aren't my notes. "All right then, thanks for your time." Tim realized that now was not the time to argue about the details. Someone had changed the notes in this case file that was certain. Again someone was protecting

Andy Morrell.

"Can I ask why you are looking into this now?"

"The case has always bothered me. I am between cases right now, so I thought I would check in to see if there was any new information. I guess not."

"I hear you, man. Sorry, I wasn't much help."

"It is what I expected. But again thanks for you time."

The two officers said good-bye promising to keep the other informed of any new information. Already Tim had broken that promise with the recent admission from the sister. The case is cold? The case is barely two years old how can it be classified as cold. The politicizing of this case had angered Tim, but this was more. Someone deliberately shut this case down and reassigned those in charge. The question was why? Andy Morrell was a nobody. What did he ever do to get such special preferential treatment? Alyssa Rowe was a relative nobody. Why go to such lengths to shut this case down? *Maybe it is not what Andy did as much as what he knows. Why not just kill him or make him disappear?*

Tim tapped his pen on the desk thinking. He dialed the research clerk's extension.

"Hi, Special Agent Tim Thibodeau how long to pull up everything on the Alyssa Rowe case?" He listened to the litany of excuses, budget cuts, how busy and short staffed he was, and it would take about an hour. "Great I'll go to lunch and come down then." Tim hung up, stood up and stretched, lunch would help to clear his head. On the way out of the building, Tim stopped at a fellow agent's desk.

"Lunch?" The other nodded, stood up grabbing the suit jacket off the back of his chair and walked out of the building with Tim.

CHAPTER TWENTY-EIGHT

The two agents walked down the street to a corner café. The café was packed with local office workers on their half hour lunch. Lucky the two walked in just as a table by the window facing the street open up. Not waiting for anyone to clear the dirty dishes the two hustled over to the table to sit down. Sitting by the window facing the street was Tim's favorite seat in the house. Tim liked to eat watching the people go about their business in the streets. The city of Bangor was not a big city by America's standards, but it had all the same mechanics of a large city. You had your small businesses, like this café, big name brand store fronts, like Ace Hardware, the people on the streets were all there for a reason. This was downtown Bangor, strictly the commercial district and not residential. There weren't even any converted apartments above the stores here like you see in other cities.

Max, the other agent, ordered a steak sandwich with fries, coleslaw, and a diet coke. Tim ordered the BLT toasted on wheat, onion rings, potato salad, and a regular coke. One of the perks of being an FBI agent were the regular physical exams to make sure that your body weight was within agency parameters. The only way to maintain the required body weight was to work out on a regular basis. Tim ran every day like clockwork. The upshot to working out every day was that Tim could pretty much eat what he wanted without worrying about gaining weight.

"So what gives, why the invite to lunch?" Max asked between bites.

"Just got a tip on the Alyssa Rowe case and I'm waiting for research to pull the case file." Tim stated casually like it was no big deal.

Max whistle and said, "Be careful the big wigs were pretty clear on that case and it could mean serious trouble for you. Why you so stuck on this one?"

"It's a little kid and the father reeks. I just can't let it go. You would think since Watergate and Nixon no FBI Administrator would risk even the hint of interfering with an official FBI investigation, but the way they are protecting Andy is beyond me." Tim replied getting himself worked up, again. Sadly, political interference in an investigation happened all the time. If you are a friend of a neighbor of a Senator, you got special treatment. For the agent, the trick was to find the evidence. Once you had the evidence then, all your friends in the world would not stop the wheels of justice. Unfortunately, this investigation was shut down before any real hard evidence could be found.

Max's phone rang, he answered and handed the phone to Tim. "It's for you."

Tim arched is eyebrows and took the phone. "Hi, this is Special Agent Tim Thibodeau."

It was the research lab calling to tell him the Rowe file was gone. It had been checked out.

"All of it?" Tim asked.

"The whole thing, sent to Washington, D.C.." The clerk placing the emphasis on *Washington, D.C.*

"What would Langley want with this?" Tim said out loud no necessarily to the research clerk.

"Not Langley. Capital Hill."

"Capital Hill? Under whose orders?" Tim responded surprised. He had never heard of an investigation going to

Capital Hill.

"It doesn't say, but they sent everything including the evidence box. All I got is an empty spot on the shelves. And get this, they took it after hours. I wasn't even on duty when they did it."

"Do you know when?"

"No, date and time are not registered. It's like the whole thing just vanished and rematerialized on Capital Hill. No one has asked to see this file since I last put it away nearly two years ago."

Max gestured holding his hand up for his partner to explain.

Tim held the receiver in one hand and said to Max. "The entire case file on Alyssa Rowe, notes, evidence, all of it has been sent to Capitol Hill."

Max was just as stunned. In all his years with the bureau, he had never heard of an open case file being sent to someone other than law enforcement. This completely violates the chain of evidence. "Who authorized this?"

"I don't know, but I intend to find out." Tim waved to the server to bring the check. The two finished their meals, paid up, and went back to the office. This time, Max joined Tim on his search for answers.

CHAPTER TWENTY-NINE

The Senator sat at her desk reading the summary notes on the latest handgun control bill. Shaking her head, *this one is worse than that last, it'll never pass.* She wondered if the authors wrote these bills in such a way to actually prevent them from passing just so they could tell their constituents that they were *tough on* crime. She chuckled, *what a joke.*

The private line in her office rang grabbing her attention. *This can't be good.* The Senator answered her phone on the second ring. Her voice was pleasant and friendly suggesting a willingness to help. The voice on the other end of the line set a chill through her entire body. Her demeanor changed noticeably as she listened to whomever on the other end of the phone. Her aide stopped walking into the room seeing the change, her aide hesitated in the doorway watching the Senator and then pulled the door closed behind her leaving the Senator alone. The aide was unnerved by the change in her boss that she stood by the doorway eavesdropping.

Sternly the Senator states, "Don't do anything yet, just watch. Let me know if anything else happens." *Click* The Senator hangs up the phone. She sits very still with her hand still touching the phone starring straight ahead. *This could be trouble,* she thinks to her self. Several minutes pass with the

Senator sitting motionless., Hearing nothing, her aide reaches for the door to enter, but changes her mind. She can come back later. Something about the Senator's reaction makes her aide uncomfortable and she decides to give the Senator some space. She turns to return to her desk when she hears the Senator on the phone. As if frozen in place, her aide continues to listen to her boss at the door.

The Senator reaches for her pocket book she pulls out her cell phone and makes a call. The phone is answered before it rings.

"Call me on a secure line." The phone goes dead before the Senator responds.

The Senator opens up her front desk draw pulling it out as far as she can and reaches into the back for a throwaway track phone. She pulls it out and realizes that it is dead. Reaching for the charger in the desk she plugs in the phone and waits until the phone turns on. She makes the call.

"What took you so long?" The voice on the other end demands.

"I had to charge the phone."

"I told you to keep that phone ready at all times."

"Kind of obvious having a phone out charging at all times."

"Whatever, what's up?"

"We got a nosey person up in the Bangor Office. He's asking about our family. Check into it for me and let me know."

"Will do," said the voice on the other end and hung up.

The Senator sat down and put her head in her hands. She massaged her temples feeling a headache coming on. *This is not a good time with elections coming up.*

The Senator sent a text message to a different number, "Agent Thibodeau is digging into the case again." She tosses the phone into her purse with the charger still connected and stands up. The Senator crosses the room to the closed door and realized that the door is not closed completely. She pulls the door open expecting to see her aide standing there, but no one is there.

Sighing to herself she relaxes knowing no one was listening to her conversation.

CHAPTER THIRTY

Sally stood watching Theresa through the window in the door of her classroom. Theresa smiled and turned to talk in the class discussion. Sally noticed that ever since the crazy meltdown in her office, Theresa seemed more relaxed, happy even. Sally tried to follow up with her about what she said, but Theresa just said she was mad at her mother and to forget about it. Sally watched the class and waited for a break in the lesson. She did not want interrupt the flow of the class.

Theresa looked up and saw Sally in the window. Their eyes met, and Sally waved for her to join her in the hall. Sally used the moment to interrupt. "Sorry for the interruption, but mind if I take Theresa for a moment?"

Theresa got up and joined Sally in the hallway the smile gone. Sally's heart sank a bit as the change took place in the girl. "Let's go to my office so I can fill you in on everything."

Neither of them spoke as the walked to Sally's office. Once inside Theresa took a seat at the table and Sally sat down next to her.

"I know that you told me to forget about what you said, I couldn't. I reported what you said to the Principal, but given that this is not a case of neglect or abuse it, she did not think the matter was reportable. I have a friend in the FBI, so I asked him to check into it, and he said he would." Sally paused and waited for a response.

Theresa sat there and let the message sink and burst into tears. She threw her arms around Sally sobbing. "Thank you so much, this has been so hard on me, and no one I could tell and when I did they didn't believe me. Thank you, Thank you, Thank you."

"Oh sweetheart, you are very welcome. No promises, but I know my friend and he will do as he says." Sally was relieved that she did what she did.

CHAPTER THIRTY-ONE

Tim sat at his desk with all his old case notes around him. In front of him, he put a yellow legal pad with the name of Andy in the middle. Now why would a man with no criminal history suddenly commit such a heinous act? Andy's world had been clean until he met that girlfriend of his. What was her name? *Karen Tanneger.* This chick was a piece of work. She was up to her eyeballs in all kinds of illegal activity and nothing ever sticks. Tim stepped into the hallway and called out.

"Max, who did the interview on Andy's girlfriend, Karen Tanneger, El Guapo's sister?"

"Dunno who did the first interview, but I was going to do a follow up interview when she lawyered up and skipped town." Looking at his notes, Max continued to recite the sequence of events. "She went back to Miami. I went to Florida to do a follow up interview, but by the time I got there she had been killed in a gang related shooting. She was not the target. She was a bystander, but was dead nonetheless and I never did get a follow up. That lead ended right there."

"Do you think it odd that a major lead would end up dead?"

"Yes and no, she ran with some really nasty folks."

Tim knew he had to get the rest of the case files. "Hey, can I file a Freedom of Information Act petition to get the case files?"

"Don't see why not. It always works when the file the petition on us."

The petition worked, and the files were ordered for release with the limitation to files that were electronic. As a result, Tim could not find any notes on the interview other than the entry log. He did however get the name of the investigator that interviewed her, Officer John LeClair Maine State Police. Time to find Officer LeClair.

CHAPTER THIRTY-TWO

The trip from Bangor to Redwood took just under two hours. Not much traffic once you got past Newport. This really was "out in the woods", for the last 20 miles there had been no gas station or grocery store. Tim took the time to review the case, especially concentrating on the irregularities. Someone had gone to a lot of trouble to make this case go away. Designating it as cold case in such a short time, witnesses gone missing, files being sent outside law enforcement, the chain of evidence completely mismanaged. The question is who has the power to make all that happen in a federal case? And then there was me. I had this information on Andy in the beginning and what did I do, nothing I chalked it up as another crazy person. It is hard enough to launch a full fledge investigation in Maine, but then to have seriously powerful people working against you, it is impossible.

The more I look at this case the more I think the girlfriend, Karen Tanneger, had a big role. Karen was a good looking woman running in social circles way beyond those of Andy Morrell. As far as we could see, Andy did not have much of a social life, living with his mother, going to a few bars here and there. How in the world did his path cross Karen's? How did a guy like Andy Morrell get the attention of a highflying lady like Karen? That connection alone made this case unusual. El Guapo, what do we know about him and how heavily involved is his sister in the family business. Tim realizes he really does not know a lot about El Guapo and makes a mental note to find out more when he gets back to the office.

Driving into the small town of Redwood, Tim was taken with the view. The full expanse of Moose Lake was laid out before him as he entered town. This was his first time here although he had wanted to come and see his friend Sally for a long time, he never had an excuse to just drop in. This town was not on the way to anything, beyond the town laid the great northern woods of Maine. The roads literally stopped here.

The town itself was not much to speak of, a trading post, a few stores, gas station, post office, all the basic necessities and not much more. The overall the impression of the town was shabby and sad. Why would his friend chose to live here it is so off the beaten path with very little to offer. The remoteness of the place made it very attractive after the terror attacks of 9/11. For a while there you couldn't buy much for under half a million dollars. Now you couldn't give your property away. Maybe that is why Sally stayed. Tim turned left at the blinking light and continued to the school.

Tim was meeting the girl at the school in Sally's office. Tim was concerned about jurisdiction and school privacy laws. The girl in question, was a minor and the required the presence of a parent during questioning. As far as Tim knew the parents were unaware of today's meeting. Sally planned to have a friendly visit with Tim and have Theresa conveniently "drop" in while he was there. Tim had deliberately worn jeans and a T-shirt today to emphasize that this was a casual meeting. His business clothing, scream G-Man. Tim pushed the buzzer on the side door of the school. He read the rules waiting for a response.

"Can I help you?" A hard voice from years of smoking, finally answered.

"I'm Tim Thibodeau. Here to see Sally." Tim replied as genial as possible. He realized that he was actually nervous about his meeting today.

Tim knew the rules about letting students meet with law enforcement, the school was obligated to contact the parents. Theresa had agreed to meet with Tim with a stipulation that her mother was not know. Tim wanted to hear what she had to say, so he agreed. So far, this was the only true lead he had in the case, a cold case that no one was investigating.

Theresa was not what he expected given the history of her mother's drug addition and havoc that must have wreaked in her life. Sally introduced the two, smiled, and left them alone in her office. Theresa told Tim everything that happened that night, how she came to be hiding in the closet, and what she heard.

"I didn't think of baby selling until much later when Alyssa's body was not found. Then I got to thinking and the man referred to the money and my sister together and so I think he was talking about baby selling." Theresa explained.

"You never got a good look at him?"

"No, I never saw him only heard part of the conversation."

"Do you think you could identify the voice if you heard it again?"

"I doubt it. I was so scared. I cannot even tell you if the other was Alyssa's dad. I always assumed it was, but I never met the guy. I don't think I even seen him speak to the reporters. Do you mind my asking, how come you guys never arrested Andy Morrell?"

"Officially, we never had enough hard evidence to make an arrest. Unofficially, he is being protected by some powerful allies."

"I'm a kid, I get that, but I thought it weird you guys just leaving him alone. My mom is always ranting conspiracy this and that and I know she is not quite all there in the head, but this I think is weird."

"You were the one who called me early in the investigation weren't you?" Tim asked the young lady.

"Yes, that was me." Theresa sighs. "I was convinced that

that one phone call would solve everything. That Alyssa would come home and everything would be fine, but it wasn't. I was so sad for so long when I realized it didn't change a thing. I also realize that I have no evidence and it is my word against two guys I never saw. I was so stupid."

"No, you are not stupid. It takes a lot of courage to make a call like that and even more courage to follow up when you know most people will not believe you. I am grateful that you were willing to speak to me today. It's not much, but it is different perspective and I think I know just where to begin digging."

Tim extended his hand to Theresa, and they shook hands.

"This is my direct line that also rings to my cell phone if I am away from my desk." Tim hands his business card to Theresa and says, "if you think of anything else or something else comes up please call no matter how inconsequential you may think it is."

"I will." Theresa leaves first and returns to her class.

Sally sees Theresa leave her office and she gives her a thumbs up, but Theresa is looking down at the ground and does not see her. Sally walks into her office and asks, "So? How did it go?"

"You know I can't talk about an ongoing investigation." Tim chided.

"I knew it!" Sally exclaimed.

CHAPTER THIRTY-THREE

The weather could not have been nicer on the drive back, clear blue skies and dry roads. Hardly any cars on the road giving Tim time to think. One hundred thousand dollars is a lot of money. To a guy like Andy, working in the mill, a hundred grand would be like winning the lottery. He had heard of people buying babies for that much, but this was a 2-year old child. Who would pay that kind of money for a toddler? Tim considered the possible implications, could there be a human trafficking in Maine? Tim calls Max. "Hey, tell me what you know about El Guapo."

"It's a lot, this is one serious bad ass dude." Max stated emphatically.

"The sister told me that she overheard a conversation about Alyssa that included the amount of one hundred thousand dollars." Tim let that hang between them.

Letting out a slow whistle, "are you thinking human trafficking?"

"You said it, not me." Tim starting to feel momentum for his new theory.

"That would tie in El Guapo. *And* that would explain the special treatment of Andy. " Shaking his head, "like I said these are some serious dudes, they got their hands in everyone's pockets. That's why he continues to operate in plain sight. Never any charges that stick."

"Any ideas on how we proceed with this theory? The investigation is a bust. Could we just look into the possibility of human trafficking without bringing the Rowe case into it? For now."

"Let me think on this and make a few calls to some friends at Langley. See you when you get here." Max hung up quickly. Max was a man on a mission.

"See you there." Tim said to dead airspace.

The rest of the drive back, Tim considered how to proceed. Human trafficking was not unheard of, but it was generally an international and was in the jurisdiction of the CIA. The minimal briefing that Tim had on the topic included the kidnapping of young runaways, male and female, and shipping them off as sex-slaves. The smuggling of humans is a mean business. With all the added security measures, getting human cargo out of the country required macabre measures. Measures that made the coyotes smuggling in aliens to be first class travel accommodations. There had been rumors inside the Bureau of human trafficking in Maine, but nothing substantial, nothing concrete. As far as Tim knew, human trafficking involved major international players, the Russian mob, Eastern European crime gangs, Asian Mobs, Middle Eastern Mobs. To play in the international human trafficking arena you had to be highly organized, well connected, and have a network of interests to move people from one country to the next. Where does El Guapo fit in with these guys? And how does a guy like Andy Morrell get involved with the likes of these guys? Where do I start? There was no question that Tim was in way over his head on this one. He was going to need to have a top-notch task force set up and to do that he needed evidence, whole lot more than the testimony of a teenager who did not want her mother to know.

CHAPTER THIRTY-FOUR

For the most part, Tyler St. Jean could not complain. He was paid a shitload of money to play on his computer all day. As a result he had a nice house, car, and life. He was provided with the very best, state of the art, computer equipment, He had access to continuous upgrades so he could do his job like no one else. He was more than just good at his job, he was somewhat of a genius. He could have become anything he wanted, but he lack discipline and school required discipline. He possessed no degrees, flunked out of community college, and was an IT nobody. Given his current employment status, being an IT nobody worked to his advantage.

He held no illusions about who he worked for or the kind of man his boss was, but he always treated him well and he gave him a job when no one else would. Tyler tried to get a job on his merits, but he couldn't even land a job as a mail clerk. He was living in his parent's basement spending his day playing video games and smoking pot. His parents yelled at him all the time and nagged at him to get off his lazy ass and get a job. He tried to get a job, but with only a high school diploma, no one wanted to hire him for a real job that would afford him the chance to move out on his own. It was gaming that he got the attention of a guy who knew a guy that got him in touch with his now current boss.

His job was to monitor the Internet, both open and the deepnet. He was looking for any mention of his boss, family, or names provide by his boss. The boss referred to these peoples as "family members". Tyler would provide familiar names for each one, like Aunt Jackie or Cousin Fred. This was useful in keeping people straight and to avoid suspicions if any Intel was intercepted. If Tyler heard any chatter he was to record it and track down the person talking. This part of the job was pretty easy and did not challenge his technological prowess. The chatter on his boss and family went in spurts. Tyler could monitor for weeks without a peep and then some days it was nonstop. Tyler assumed it had to do with work dealings, but given the nature of his boss' profession it was better to not know the full circumstances. Sometimes, he was asked to do some minor hacking or spying that went beyond Internet monitoring. He particularly enjoyed these little extra assignments. They challenged his thinking and technical savvy because rule number one is to not get caught. His relative obscurity in terms of industry experts allowed him to come and go in the digital reality of cyberspace with no one being the wiser.

Tyler tagged all the major search engines with a specific search sequence that would send him an alert when anyone typed in the name of a "family member". This was a Tyler original a search to search the search engines. The beauty of the programing was its flexibility, he could update with whenever he needed.

Ping. Someone was doing a Boolean search on some distant relatives. Time to get to work. Tyler began typing on the keyboard and let out a whistle when he saw that the search was not for one family member, but two *in combination!* Typing more rapidly, Tyler pauses and scribbles on his notepad. Whoever is searching is not searching from a home office, this server had serious firewalls and security. Tyler got up and walked around the room asking himself, "who in Bangor has this kind of IT security? A bank? A bank, a bank, a bank." Tyler was pacing and talking out loud, "there are no banks in Bangor with that kind of security, the only one in Bangor would be, would be," Tim walked back and forth and then stopped, he got it. "The FBI, The Fucking Bureau of Investigations!" Tyler sat down and began typing. He sat back and smiled. *It's the FBI.* Reaching for his phone book he looked up the Bangor office of the FBI and there it was. He smiled again. *All that security and they list their field officers in the phone book, incredible.* Tyler did a quick search combing the names El Guapo and Alyssa Rowe to see what that combination produced. He found one hit on the sister being involved with Alyssa's dad. Not bad considering he knew what he was searching for and could not find it online.

Tyler picked up his cell phone and sent a text, "FBI is searching for a relationship between our Florida relation and our Waterville relation. The agents are listed in the phonebook." Tyler put down his phone and sat back staring at the screen. *Looks like it's about to get interesting* Tyler smiled. No sooner did he have that thought when his computer chimed again, this time two words, "human trafficking."

CHAPTER THIRTY-FIVE

David struggled to write the summary of the proposed legislation, the extention of the Medicaid program by increasing the income threshold to 138% of the poverty level. This would double the number of participants. The first three years are to be fully funded by the federal government and then it would be up to the individual states to make up the difference. *This state is already broke, how can anyone consider expanding* welfare. The bill on many level bothered him and he was finding it difficult to write an impartial report for the Senator. David pushed away from his desk and stood to stretch. He thought that maybe a coffee in the cafeteria would help him to refocus and get this assignment done.

David reached for his jacket off the back of his chair and put it on smoothing out the lapel. The dress code demanded that men where jacket and tie everyday, no casual Fridays in this line of work. David owed exactly two jackets and so he was careful to keep them from getting soiled. David put his hand on the door handle when her heard the familiar chimed on the Senator's computer. The first time this had happened, David panicked thinking his computer was crashing. David stood motionless debating about whether to get the computer or the cup of coffee. The computer won out as David's sense of duty trumped the coffee.

A string of names scrolled down the screen: *Maxwell*

Weiss, Alyssa Rowe, El Guapo, Karen Tanneger, and Timothy Thibodeau. David jotted down the names as quickly as he could not sure he had gotten all of them. Like the last time, the message scrolled down and then disappeared returning to the normal login page. David had made some inquiries with the technology team about who would set up such an alarm system and was told that what he described was not possible.

Looking at the list David recognized some of the names. Wondering what the connection was between the list of names to each other and the Senator, David walked the phone message to the Senator's desk and left it in the middle. *Now for that cup of coffee* David sighed and left the office.

CHAPTER THIRTY-SIX

The Senator needed a place to be alone and think. Her past was catching up with her and it was getting out of control. She felt reasonably confident she had stalled the FBI investigation, but the mother. The mother kept calling press conferences and demanding action. The public opinion was swayed by these rants and raves and her office would get the demand for action. *Maybe if you weren't such a lousy mother your kid would be safe and sound at home.*

The Senator pulled her government issued car into the staff only parking lot. There were a couple of cars in the lot, but not many. The building was usually quite quiet on Sundays. Being a senior senator she had a parking spot close to the building. She walked in breathing in the cool autumn air, smells like snow. About time we had snow, so far it has been a mild start to winter. Walking into the building could feel the quiet. She took the stairs, not trusting the elevator in this ancient building, especially with the place so vacant. She could end up spending the night in the elevator before anyone knew she was here. The main staircase was made of worn granite that curved to a balcony on the second floor. During the week this staircase was much too busy to bother with, but today it was a nice break to walk the steps that so many before had walked. The domed ceiling was painted a pale yellow color without mural or design, giving the whole entrance, a warm sunny feel, even in winter. She considered herself lucky to have space in the state capital, most states your federal office was a storefront in a major state town or towns across the state depending on how big your state was. Here in Maine you get to share the government buildings free of charge. You could hear the sounds of the building, the rattling of the old steam pipes working to keep the building passably warm. The Senator often retreated to the office on Sunday because she knew no one would think to look for her there, and she could be alone.

Her situation was getting out of hand, too many people were poking their noses where they did not belong. Rationalizing her actions, she told herself that the kid was better off. She just did not know how to contain the continued interest in the case. The kid was gone, end of story. *Why couldn't they just get on with their lives?* Kids disappear all the time. Kids die. Kids get abducted.

Taking her coat off as she entered her office through a separate entrance just for her. This way she could avoid running into anyone working in her office and just be in *her inner sanctuary*. She stopped as she stood in her office listening to any sounds that her Aide was working today. She was relieved to her only silence in return, she sat down in her chair heaving a sigh of relief. *I just have to wait this out.* "This too will pass, and all will be right with the world," she told herself enjoying the solitude.

Staring at the center of her desk, she saw the phone message with list of names.. Grabbing the message while leaping to her feet she exclaimed, "What the Fuck!"

Recognizing her Aide's handwriting, she racked her brains to figure out how David could possibly know these names. Scanning the list mouthing the names as she went, *Maxwell Weiss, Alyssa Rowe, El Guapo, Karen Tanneger, and Timothy Thibodeau.* David was always such a good kid, *is he blackmailing me?* "Think damn it!" She said aloud. Pacing back and forth and realized that since this was a phone message, someone must have called her with these names. Something is afoot and to make this call they must be getting very close to her connection. *Think, what have you done so far? You shut down the*

FBI investigation and you... Oh My God! What if they know that I am the one? What if they know why?

She grabbed her phone and snapped a picture of the message. She texted the picture to her source stating, "this was left for me – take care of it!" No smiley face on this one. The Senator sat down at her desk just staring at her phone waiting for some divine answer. She did not know how long she sat there, but it was getting dark outside. Feeling worse than when she came in she considered getting a room nearby, but scrap the idea since she did not have a change of clothes or even a toothbrush. She slowly got up and made her way to her car and driving the two hours home to the coast.

CHAPTER THIRTY-SEVEN

Special Agents Weiss and Thibodeau were working hard to create a diagram of all the interested parties. The connections that they were able to build by just adding El Guapo to the list of "known associations." Of course El Guapo was merely a theory, but by using this name in connection to all the other known names in the Alyssa Rowe case began to take form in a whole new direction. Using the white board in the main conference room the two made a diagram of all the connections they had uncovered so far with Alyssa position in the center. The scene surfacing on the white board looked like a web that children use to study a single concept, everything related to each other in some way or another. Standing back and looking at the board both agents had the same thought without voicing it. *How could we have missed this?*

"Jeez, this thing has ties to the Odessa family, State and Federal Politician." Max whistle through his teeth shaking his head. "We really need to take a look at other missing children for what the past five maybe ten years."

"Agree" Tim stated just as incredulous as Max. "This explains the high power attorney and special handling."

The entire board was a hypothetical work of fiction with

all roads leading to on Yuri Mikhailov the reputed boss of the Odessa Family based in Brighton Beach, New York.

"What can we prove?" Tim asked. He knew without evidence they would never be able to get Alyssa's case moved out of cold storage.

"Not a God damn thing." Max said shaking his head.

"Let's work the other way. What do we know about each of these people and their possible motives for being involved?"

Max pointed to Senator Jane Schmidt. "Take the Senator here, she ran on a small town girl, plain Jane image, but look at the campaign financing. She consistently runs some of the most expensive campaigns in this State's history. Where is she getting the money? She is not wealthy on her own and her husband certainly does not have that kind of money."

"You think this is all about money?" Tim asked.

"It's always about money, sooner or later it always comes down to money. People kid themselves into believing in some high and mighty reasons, but take away the money, take away the motive."

"Okay, so where does Alyssa Rowe fit in or her family for that matter?"

"Russian mafia, Odessa Family involved, my bets on human trafficking." Max said it so matter-of-factly it sent a chill down Tim's spine. *This was Maine for crying out loud, we take care of one another we don't sell our children to the highest bidder. Do we?* Tim screamed in his head.

"Where does El Guapo fit into all this?"

"I am still working on that. So far, I cannot find the connection. I'm almost thinking that he is not involved at all. Besides, we are talking about people in a position to shut down an FBI investigation." Max said picking El Guapo's photo off the table.

"I don't buy coincidences, why on Earth would Karen Tanneger go out with Andy Morrell? Did you get a good look at her? She had a reason to be dating Andy and it was not love." Tim said taking the photo from Max. "Tell me what you know old man." Tim asked of the photo of El Guapo.

"If only it were that simple. We still don't have anything to open up this investigation." Max responded defeated.

CHAPTER THIRTY-EIGHT

The drive to Rosewood took just shy of five hours, but you landed in the middle of nowhere. It was a straight shot up I-95 until you reached Newport and then it was very slow going the rest of the way meandering through one horse towns, waiting for slow moving log trucks. The Appalachian Trail cut through somewhere near here and the last 15 miles all you see are hikers. *Doesn't anyone have a job?*

The view as you came into town was nothing less than spectacular. The town is nestled in a small valley on the edge of Maine's largest inland lake, Coming into town from the south there is a large trading post that sits at the top of the hill where you can see the entire town sitting on the edge of one of Maine's most beautiful lakes. From the top of the hill, the town is dotted with cute coastal building along the edge and you can see the spires of the church steeple. For the man this was not the first time he had seen the view and yet it still took his breath away.

On further inspection of the town, the initial quaintness gave way to the sorely neglected shabbiness of the buildings. The missing shutters and peeling paint told the story of a town facing its share of financial difficulties. The stark loneliness of the vacant buildings and shops stood as testaments to the hard times being faced by the people of Redwood. There were a few cars parked along the street, mostly pick-ups, suggesting that these vehicles belong to the locals who most likely worked in the shops and not customers shopping.. On the one and only real corner of town, stood a store with the name "Indian Store and Gift Shop", the name was so politically incorrect that the man chuckled to himself thinking that only this far out could you name your store the Indian Store and not have protesters out front picking you. Through the window of the store, the man could see what looked like a second hand junk shop. Tempted to pull over and check out the inside and see who owned the place, the man continued on. He reminded himself that he was here to do a job.

The man already knew the place he was looking for and it was up just a little ways past the center of town. A sign boasting the "best Gumbo in town" was where he was headed. Again the comical side of himself wondered just how many places served gumbo in this town to be considered the "best", more than likely the sign should read, "the Only Gumbo in town."

Walking into the place, the man was confident no one would remember him from his previous visit, not that kind of place. There were a few locals seated at the bar who bothered to look up briefly as he entered and then turned back to their own business. *This is the perfect spot, people here, yet no one interested enough to ask me any questions.* Looking at his watch he notes that it is just after two pm giving him just enough time. *Moose Pub, cute name too bad it ended at the name.* He and takes a seat at table with a view of the school. The bartender calls out to him about what he wants from the bar without bothering to move closer to him. He picks up a menu on the table and orders bowl of chili and a Gooseneck beer on tap. He had no intention of drinking, but judging by the other patrons in the place ordering a soft drink would draw unwanted attention.

"What's the rule about smoking?" He asks the bartender.

"Take it outside" she barks pointing to the front door.

The man grabs his beer and heads outside to smoke. He slowly pours half of the drink out on the ground while smoking his cigarette. He spots the girl as she walks past the bar. He compares the girl walking by with a picture on his phone. It's her all right. Putting out his cigarette her enters the bar and drops a twenty-dollar bill on the table and leaves out the back door following Theresa as she walks home.

CHAPTER THIRTY-NINE

David is surprised to find the Senator in the office when he arrives on Monday morning. Immediately he is a bundle of nerves at her presence. It feels as if she was waiting for him.

"Good Morning David. Thought I get some work done from my home office." The Senator smiles.

"Good Morning to you, can I get you anything?"

"A cut of Tea, if it's not too much trouble." The Senator watches David's reaction. He seems nervous that I am here. "Do you like working here?" The Senator asks.

"Very much so," David replies. "I'll get that tea for you. What do you take in your tea?"

"One sugar." The Senator smiles and heads for her office.

David heads downstairs to the cafeteria. He was counting the times he had actually worked in the same office with the Senator and he was thinking that this was the only time. He knew she came in after hours as evident by her work, or notes she would leave for him, but actually working with her in her presence. *Nope, not ever before.*

David quietly enters the Senator's office and places the tea on the corner of her desk.

"It seems really quiet." The Senator says almost

rhetorically or to the walls and not to David at all.

"It's still early. I am usually one of the first Aides to show up in the building."

David realizes he was still in his coat. He was distracted with finding the Senator here and then going to get her tea, he did not notice he had not taken his coat off. His lunch was sitting on top of his desk. There was a coat rack by the door for visitors, but David usually put his coat in the supply closet. David had a morning ritual that he followed every morning, but today he was off and had to stop and think about what he need to do first. David headed for the supply closet and took off his coat and boots and put them away and cross the room in his stocking feet. The Senator was sitting at her desk watching him the whole time. David grabbed his shoes out of the lower draw of the cabinet next to his desk.

David plopped down in his chair expelling the breath he did not know he was holding and went to work putting on his shoes.

"David, where is my computer?" The Senator called from her desk.

"It's out here at my desk . The tech guys swapped them out a couple of weeks ago when mine crashed, this close to the election they said they could not go around replacing hardware." The Senator chuckled. "Do you want me to call them and have them put it back." David called out to her in response. He was talking too fast and explaining too much.

"No, I've got my laptop with me. I just noticed it missing."

The initial shock of having his boss in the office today gave way to the work that had to be done. The fact that the Senator was here doubled David's workload. David pulled up the Senator's schedule on his computer and looked to see if any of the meetings could be rerouted to this office.

Stepping to the door David asked, "Do you want me to reroute your meetings for today?"

"See what is a priority, what can be rerouted, and what needs to be reschedule for a later date." The Senator said all business like.

David quickly got to work. He worked the phone, calling constituents explaining that there had been a change in the schedule and that the Senator was in Augusta today. All but one person on today's appointment list could come to Augusta. The one person who could not come into Augusta was fine with a phone meeting. David felt a sense of pride that he was able to keep all of the Senator's appointments without having to reschedule a single one, rescheduling was such a nightmare. David worked hard to set up the conference room with the necessary amenities. Since he never held meetings in this office, he was not sure of what beverages he should supply, so he went a little overboard to make sure everyone was happy. *This sure beats stuffing envelopes*, David smiled at the thought. David was excited to be able to work so closely with the Senator, this was the reason that he took this job, he respected the Senator's politics and admired the way she handled her business. This was not just some job to David, he was a real fan.

The Senator watched her Aide work. He was very efficient and did not mention the phone message. She was debating on whether to bring it up or not. On one hand, what David knew was critical to the Senator and on the other hand, if he knew nothing then she did not want to pique his curiosity.

While waiting for the first meeting, the Senator approached her Aide and thanked him for his work today. She broached the subject of the phone message by asking how everything was going in the office and whether or not there were any oddities. David said all was pretty much routine, but that the building lost power a few days ago and the generators kicked in. The Senator was confident that her Aide was not blackmailing her, but did not understand where he got the list of names on the phone message.

"There was a weird phone message on my desk..." The Senator started.

"My thoughts exactly, it was a list of names that came through on the computer screen and then disappeared. I almost called, but didn't think it was an emergency." David interrupted the Senator.

"What do you mean it "came through" the computer?"

"There was a beep sound like an alarm and then the list scrolled across the screen like a marquee. There was another similar message on the day of the power outage, but with the power outage happened I did not have a chance to write down the message. I assumed the loss of power erased the message." David lied. David did not write down the first message, but he remembered the name, but was hesitant to admit knowing at this late a date. "Do the names mean anything?"

"Not to me, maybe it was some kind of glitch or malware." The Senator answered quickly, a little too quickly.

David shrugged and was about to say something when the first appointment arrived. He directed the Senator to her first guest. David got the sense that the Senator was lying but did not know why or what it meant.

CHAPTER FORTY

The federal databases are the best for research. David got a thrill doing research on the names that had scrolled across his screen the other day. Boolean searches were the best for finding relationships between terms. David starting typing the string of names *Maxwell Weiss, Alyssa Rowe, El Guapo, Karen Tanneger, and Timothy Thibodeau.*

The fan on the computer kicked on making a whirling sound as soon as David hit the return key. The sound made it seems as if the computer was actually hard at work, thinking and searching out the names looking for connections.

The computer began to find hits that included all of the names, which surprised David. Apparently, someone else had conducted a similar search with the same combination of names. The search results did not indicate any relationships between the names just that this was not the first search with this combination. David scratched his head thinking what to do next and decided to put each name separately and see if he could find a connection or an anchor. An anchor is a search term or key word, that all seem to have in common. The anchor holds the search together in the same manner that an anchor holds a ship in place.

That worked all of them had Alyssa Rowe and Timothy Thibodeau as anchors. Weird to have two anchors in any given search., you were lucky to find one. Timothy Thibodeau is an

Agent for the FBI. Maybe everyone is connected to him through his casework or maybe through the same case? Did Agent Thibodeau investigate the Alyssa Rowe case? That would be the most logical conclusion, everyone on this list is connected to the FBI investigation of Alyssa Rowe. That would explain the two anchors. David knew enough about computers to realize that the Senator's explanation of how the names ended on her computer did not make sense. *Computer glitches do not produce lists of names, nonsense yes, but names of real people, who are now somehow all connected. This was a deliberate message, but what does this have to do with the Senator?*

David brought up the files on Alyssa Rowe. *Wow, how sad. How come the father was never arrested? What does the Senator have to do with this?* With those questions in mind, David began digging through the electronic information in front of him. Wow again, David thought get a load of who the attorney is representing the father. That name meant a lot to David. As a matter of fact, Jeff Petersen was the meeting yesterday that was done on the phone. Jeff Petersen was the Senator's attorney and campaign finance manager. David looked into Andy Morrell background and the more he dug, the more convinced that there was no way that he just hired Jeff Petersen on his own. That Law Firm would never have returned a call from the likes of Andy Morrell, let alone agree to represent him.

David began to paint a picture of all the connections. Timothy Thibodeau and Maxwell are both FBI agents presumably working on the Alyssa Rowe case. Karen Tanneger is El Guapo's sister and Karen Tanneger is the girlfriend of Andy Morrell. Andy Morrell is Alyssa Rowe's biological father and the connection to the Senator is Jeff Petersen, the attorney. But why the warning and why did the Senator lie about the names? Given the list of names, David was confident that the Senator was behind Andy Morrell getting Jeff Petersen to represent him, *why on earth would the Senator become involved with the likes of Andy Morrell?* The why was well beyond his pay grade or intellectual comprehension.

David cleverly set up an alert on his computer to notify him of anyone searching these names in combination with one another and individually. There is no privacy when it comes to the Internet. All the major search engines routinely kept records of searches including user IP addresses, date and time of searches. When David was done, he pushed back from the computer pleased with his work. What David did not realize was that someone else had already set up a similar alert and was currently tracking his IP Address.

CHAPTER FORTY-ONE

For the first time in his life, David felt that he was actually doing something productive. He did not know what he was doing, but he knew that the names on that list were important. They were important to the Senator and to the family of Alyssa Rowe. With the alert in place, David packed up for the day to go home. Tomorrow morning he would know if anyone else was investigating these individuals too, but more importantly if anyone was investigating any combination of these people.

David's home was a rented studio apartment walking distance to the capitol. Augusta's main district was a small with a lot of old buildings. The apartment was in and older building in need of serious repairs if not outright demolition. The downstairs section of the apartment was currently rented to a shop that sold a variety of tourist items from syrup to t-shirts. There was one boiler for the whole building located in the back of the store. The furnace was inefficient, which translated to David never had enough heat in the winter. In order for David to get enough heat, the store turned into a hothouse. The fact that the boiler was located in the store translated to the only thermostat was also located in the store. David had no control over the heat or when, he believed that during the day while he was at work there was plenty of heat, but at night he was sure the old bat downstairs shut if off.. David would talk with the shop owner from time to time and explain that he was really cold at night, which would help for a while, but then it would go back to being really cold in the apartment when he got home after work. On the weekends when the shop was open, David was never cold during the day proving his theory that the shop owner turned it up during the day and off at nights. The rent was perfect at three hundred a month heat included.

The best part of David's apartment is the view. The front windows looked out over the capitol with no obstructions. David had made a sitting area in front of the windows and on weekends he spent a lot of time sitting there reading or working. Like other small towns in Maine, Augusta rolls up its sidewalks by nine and by ten o'clock in the evening the downtown was a ghost town.

David entered his apartment like any other day and sensed something was wrong. He immediately checked the closets and bathroom, but did not find anything unusual. The studio apartment was almost one thousand square feet of living that David had divided up with the use of furniture. David had considered constructing walls, but he was not that handy and could not afford to hire anyone. David walked around the apartment and everything seemed to be in its place, and then he noticed a light on his bedside table was turned on. David must have forgotten to turn off the light this morning and it had caught his attention.

David shrugged his shoulders wondering how he missed turning off the light. He stripped his clothes off as he headed toward the bathroom leaving a trail of clothes as he hopped into the shower. David began to sing in the shower.

As soon as the man heard the shower door close he crawled out from under the bed and quietly slipped out of the apartment, leaving behind a couple of hidden cameras. One camera in the overhead light, one in the bedside lamp, and one by the sitting room, there were enough cameras to view the entire space all with audio. Except for the bathroom, the man could see and hear everything in the apartment.

The man crossed the street to a street front café and took

a window seat by the street. The waitress casually wandered over to ask what he would like. The man ordered a BLT on white toast with fries and a coke. Taking out his IPhone and sticking ear buds in his ears, the man was able to watched and listen to everything in David's apartment. To anyone else in the restaurant it looked like the man was watching a movie or a game.

CHAPTER FORTY-TWO

Tim arrived at the airport a good two hours before his flight. The Bangor Airport boasts 4 gates and a parking lot capable of parking fifty thousand cars plus. The parking lot is nearly empty and Tim pulls into a spot in long-term parking that is practically across the street to the terminal. The cost for long -term parking is two dollars per day or ten dollars for the parking garage. Laugh all you want about Bangor International Airport, it was really a very nice airport to travel out of, no lines, easy cheap parking, and no stress. Wait until he gets to Miami, that will be a nightmare compared to this. Tim was not a big fan of flying. It wasn't that he had a fear of flying, just a dislike. He did not like the feeling of being cooped up in a tin can with little to see and nothing to do. He did not enjoy talking to strangers in a the casual way that fellow travelers felt obliged to do, he did not like to read, and he certainly could not sleep on a plane. Tim would much rather drive or take a train where he could see the scenery as he past by. In a plane, all he could see was a whole lot of nothing.

Tim walks up to the counter and checks in. The woman at the airline counter is maybe early thirties and very pleasant. Tim can't help flirting with her a little. It has been so long since Tim had a date outside of work. He asks questions about the flight stalling his time with the clerk. She smiles handing Tim his boarding pass and ID, "Gate 2B upstairs and to the right."

Tim smiles back to the clerk and hands her his business

card, "Maybe you would like to go to dinner sometime?" She takes the card and smiles. "When I get back of course."

"When are you planning to be back in town?" She asks surprising Tim.

"By the end of the week, next week at the latest." Tim replies hopeful.

"Well, I'll be seeing you then Mr. Timothy." She says with a very sexy lilt in her voice and smiles.

Tim is giddy at the prospect of a date and cannot keep a grin off his face as he climbs the stairs two at time to the second floor. Tim decides to head through security right away, there are shops and restaurants on other side of the security checkpoint. It used to be that once through security there was nothing, not even a bathroom, but due to so many complaints from travelers, the airports moved the security checkpoints to include all the shops and amenities. It was a smart move on the part of the airport, it encouraged travelers to get through security earlier and not wait until the last moment and it was a boon the businesses . The shops and restaurants now have a captive audience trying to pass the time without worrying about having enough time to get through security allowing them to shop and eat all they wanted. The incidents of passengers missing their flights because they were held up in long security lines when way down and so did customer complaints, win-win all around.

Tim boards Allegiant Air Flight 920 nonstop to Miami International Airport. He's seat number is 16A and so far he does not appear to have any company in his row. He's seat is by the window and he pulls down the shade. The glare of the sun off the wings is too much for him. He looks around the plane and realizes it is about half full. Miami is not that popular in the summer months. *I bet this plane is packed during the winter.* The flight attendant begins her spiel about airplane safety and Tim half-heartedly follows along with the information card he pulled out of the seat pocket in front of him. For once Tim is not thinking about work, but that cute little brunette at the ticket counter. He realizes he never even got her name. He was surprised at the intensity of his desire to have her call him.

The plane pushes away from the gate and taxis to the runway. Tim can feel the uneven pavement under the wheels of the plane as it bounces along the taxiway. Like all roads in Maine, this one was in need of repairs. The winters are brutal and leave its mark on everything in this state long after the snow melts. The plane turns and the captain announces for the flight attendance to make ready for takeoff. Tim feels himself being pushed into the seat as the plane speeds down the runway and takes flight. *When you think about it, it is really amazing that these huge metal objects can fly.* Pushing up the shade, Tim looks out the window and the Atlantic Ocean. He can see boats and marvel at the vast expanse of the ocean. The plane continues to climb and fly through the clouds until all he can see is white obscuring the ground below until they fly through to the other side. All he can see now, is blue skies above and white puffy clouds below.

With nothing to see or do, Tim reaches into his briefcase and pulls the file on Karen Tanneger. The file is thin, not a lot of information here. She died before she could be interviewed in earnest. Staring at the photo of Karen and her brother he can see the family resemblance. *They could be twins! What is the connection?*

Tim stared ahead of him at the back of the seat in front of him. He was at a complete loss of how a Miami drug lord was involved with a missing child in Maine. The connection had to be the Russian Mob, but damn if he could find the connection. Tim longed to a cigarette at this moment. He had not smoked a cigarette in years, but right now, on this plane he wanted to light up. Smoking was no longer permitted on any airplane, for that matter smoking was no longer permitted in most places and for good reasons too. His inability to smoke at work was the biggest reason he quit. Tim sighed audibly and caught the attention of the flight attendant who made her way down the aisle to him.

"Can I get you something?" The flight attendant asked.

"Just trying to figure out a problem, thanks." Tim smiled and put his file back into his briefcase.

Tim sat in his seat thinking of the likelihood that Andy and Karen would ever meet. Karen's death was too coincidental and that bothered him. He did not know if Karen's death was an accident or not, but his gut told him it was no accident. There are some truths in law enforcement, and one of them is that there are no coincidences. Someone benefited by Karen's demise, he just wish he knew who. *What did you know?* Tim silently asked Karen's ghost.

Tim looked at the photo of the brother, Martin Prieto, AKA El Guapo. He was an attractive man on the slender side. His eyes were bright and intelligent. Absent was the hardness or cynicism one would expect with a major crime boss. This guy looked like he could be a bank president or a CEO of some fortune 500. He should be taking his lunches at the country club. This is the kind of man that should have some supermodel on his arm going out with a celebrity crew.

Tim was surprised that Martin agreed to meet with him. Of course he made it clear that he would only discuss his sister. Frankly, he was shocked that he had actually spoken to the man. Tim assured him that his interest was in his sister and her relationship with Andy Morrell. Martin agreed to meet him at his office in Miami apologizing that he was not in a position to travel as freely as he would like. Tim thanked him and said it was no problem for Tim to come to Miami. Officially Tim had taken vacation days because the investigation was not within the FBI jurisdiction. The only person who knew his real reasons for this trip was his partner, Max. *All depends on what El Guapo tells me.*

CHAPTER FORTY-THREE

Martin Prieto, the infamous drug lord, El Guapo, was officially an importer of fruit from his home country of Colombia and other South American countries. The office was the top floor of a high-rise building right on the beach, strange location for a produce company's main office. The "office" was decorated as a home and Tim wondered if this was where Martin lived when in Miami. The details were unimportant, but the place was impressive. The floors were white marble with an open floor concept. The perimeter of the room was a wall of window providing a stunning view of the Gulf of Mexico as well as Miami in both directions.

Tim was invited to sit down on a choice of cream color leather couches. He was offered a drink. Tim asked for a lemonade. While he waited for his host, Tim surveyed his surroundings. The space was opulent, but not gaudy. Tim did not know his art very well, but he was certain he was looking at original priceless paintings on the wall. He was almost certain that the one on the wall behind him was a Chagall. It reminded him of the statue at the Federal Plaza in Chicago when he was stationed there in the early part of his career. A cheese, sausage, fruit platter appeared on the coffee table in front of him. Tim reached over and helped himself, he realized he had not eaten anything today with his plane trip and all.

His host walked into the room wearing white Bermuda shorts and golf shirt. The photo did not do him justice. He was a very attractive, soft-spoken man. He was about five foot eight slender, but muscular build obviously fit and ready for anything. His dark hair was cut short, but thick and wavy. His dark eyes sparkled with a keen intellect. Tim could feel the regal air that this man commanded by his mere presence.

"Sorry to keep you waiting I was on the phone with my mother. She is inconsolable about Karen and blames me for not looking out for her. Please accept my apologies."

Tim was taken off guard by the personal admission. Tim rose and held out his hand to introduce himself.

"I am Special Agent Timothy Thibodeau, Tim. I am sorry for your loss."

"The name is Martin, Paulo Martin" El Guapo extended his hand and shook Special Agent Thibodeau's hand. "How can I help you?"

"I have reasons to believe that your sister's death was not an accident."

"My sentiments exactly. We may be on opposite sides, but I will do what I can to help my sister."

"I am on a fishing expedition. I am trying to understand the connection between your sister and Andy Morrell."

"My sister and I were very close, twins actually, but she did not confide in me about her love life."

"I'd like to get access to her personal belongings to see what I can find."

"I'll give you access to her things, but I want us to agree that this is about finding Karen's killer and not about building a case against me."

"Agreed." Tim held out his hand as a gesture of good faith.

Martin shook hands with the FBI agent thinking what strange bedfellows a personal tragedy makes. Martin signal to one of his men and whispered something in his ear. "Now if you don't mind, I have a company to run." Martin started walking out of the room and his associate he had given some kind of orders to walked Tim to the door.

Tim turned around at the door and asked Martin, "Do you know anything about why the Odessa family would be involved in this?"

Martin responded, "Not a thing. Why do you ask?" He sounded confident, but Tim saw something in his expression that was akin to alarm.

"Not sure, but the family keeps popping up in my investigation." Tim exaggerated his findings. In fact, the Odessa family's name had shown up only once in all of his attempt to connect all parties involved with this case.

CHAPTER FORTY-FOUR

David pulled into his assigned parking spot. Looking around the empty parking lot, David noted only one other car. He was earlier than usual and hoping to get a start on his day. He hoped that the Senator would be working in this office again. David grabbed his briefcase and lunch and headed into the staff only entrance of the capitol. Looking around him as he walked, David had an odd sensation. The hair on the back of David's neck tickled him as if he was being watched. Looking around and seeing only one other car in the lot, David chuckled aloud and continued his walk into the building. *Who would bother watching him. Better yet, why would anyone bother to watch him?*

David quickly dispensed of his coat and lunch and sat down at his desk. Opening the Senator's schedule for the day, David realized that the Senator had no plans of being at this office today. David's heart sank a bit and realized how disappointed he was not having the Senator here with him today. He had enjoyed working directly with her. During the down time between appointments, he had had a chance to really talk with her and get to know her as a person. He admired his boss, but did not realize how much he liked her. She was witty and smart and she made him feel so good about himself. She made him feel like he was the absolute best of all her Aides. She had asked him a lot of personal questions like she really was interested in him as a person and not some guy that worked for her.

Sighing, David turned back to his work for today, but first he wanted to check on his search from the list of names. A few strokes of the keyboard and David was able to see that his hunch was correct. The common thread was the attorney, Jeff Peterson or rather the Law Office of Wally, Habermash, and Frederickson.

David sat taping his fingers on the keyboard, thinking. *What does this have to do with the Senator?* David had a thought, but it was a long shot. Typing a few keystrokes more, David cross-referenced the names with campaign contributions to the Senator. Using the search feature of the PDF, David cross-reference campaign contributions with the Wally, Habermash, and Frederickson and clients of Wally, Habermash, and Frederickson. Campaign finance rules limited the amount that any one faction could contribute to a candidate. Maine still believed in the one-person one vote idea and was cautious about allowing the use of Super PAC to funnel huge amounts of money into one person's campaign. His search highlighted quite a few names. He began to tallying the total amount. Breathing out through his teeth David pushed away from the desk and stood up. Immediately he began to pace back and forth running his hand through his hair.

"Shit!" He swore out loud. "Damn it, damn it, damn it." *Okay think, get a hold of yourself! Maybe the Senator does not know.*

David sat back down in front of the computer and tallied the money, roughly twenty-six million dollars. *Worse case scenario?* "Worse case scenario is that they are all from the same donor with these shysters as a front. Thinking of a way to check David reached for the phone and began to call the individual donors on the list.

"May I speak with Mrs. Deborah Gould?"

"Whom may I ask is calling?"

"This is Senator Richardson's office. Are you Mrs. Gould?"

"Yes, how may I help you?"

"We are campaigning again and were hoping that you could help us out with the same donation as last year."

"I don't give to donations to politicians, you must be mistaken."

"Perhaps it was your husband?"

"I'm a widow. He's been dead for several years."

"I am terribly sorry for your loss and for bothering you." David hung up the phone without saying good-bye. As if on autopilot, David began calling the other donors on the list. Each one had a story and all of them were certain that they did not make any contribution of the Senator's campaign.

Sitting back in his chair and staring at the numbers before him, David felt sick to his stomach. These guys were the sum total of the Senator's campaign finance. They owned her and it was completely illegal. Minimally the Senator would have to resign, but depending on how much she knows, she could go to jail. David reflected on the last couple of days. David felt a myriad of emotions and the anxiety inside him was reaching a critical level. *What does all of this have to do with Alyssa Rowe?*

David got up and went to the door. He peered out into the hallway. It was mostly deserted a few of the same busy buddy faces sharing the same sorry stories. Realizing that it looked odd with him standing in the doorway, he decided he needed to take a walk. Stepping out into the hallway sent the busy buddies back into their respective offices. David continued to the elevator and decided to visit the cafeteria. David had no idea what he should do or who he could tell. David caught movement out of the corner of his eye. When he turned to get a good look there was nothing there. *Great now I am seeing things! Too much screen time, my eyes are playing tricks on me.*

David was lost in thoughts of the Senator, Alyssa Rowe, and all that money! He was so deep in his thoughts he paid no attention to anything around him. He did not notice the man enter the elevator behind him. David was so close to making a connection he could feel it. He was experiencing the same sensation of having it just on the tip of his tongue. He could feel the truth, he was so close to making the connection. At the third floor, the man brushed against him getting off the elevation. David did not feel the man slipped a piece of paper into jacket pocket.

David rode the elevator to the basement and went to the cafeteria. David grabbed a piece of pie and coffee without really thinking about it. Pushing his tray along the rails he reached the cashier. As he reached into his pocket to pull out his money, he found the note. David's heart stopped as he read, *Better watch yourself WE ARE.*

CHAPTER FORTY-FIVE

Robert Thornton, FBI Station Chief, Bangor, Maine, the title was a whole lot of nothing since nothing really interesting ever happened in Maine. Oh there was a lot of fallout from the 9/11 terrorists, but that quickly became Homeland Security's deal. No, Agent Thornton was here because they, the agency, no longer had a need for him. He had given his life to the agency and had no family as a result. He had no intention of retiring, so the agency put him "out to pasture" so to speak. In his glory days, Agent Robert Thornton had been some kind of amazing agent. He worked some impressively high profile cases, you would never know it now by looking at him, but those days were long gone.

Agent Thornton was emotionally revived with the Rowe case. He was excited with the prospects of working an actual serious case. As station chief, his role is to oversee the bureaucracy and make sure that all of his agents had what they needed to get the job done. It felt good to have a serious case to solve and then it was gone. The change in jurisdiction from the feds to local law enforcement had been incredulous. This was a missing child case and there was no way of knowing if the child had been transported across state lines or international ones for that matter. That fact alone made this a federal investigation. That had been the exact same argument that had been used to insist that this investigation was a local jurisdiction case. Agent Thornton had tried to reason that his department had more expertise and resources than any state agency, but that fell on deaf ears. In the case of missing children the first 72 hours are critical. Statistically the first 72 hours is the window when you are most likely to recover the child alive. After that, the odds of finding the child alive drop to almost zero. The handling of the Rowe girl troubled him. It had rotten stench dirty politics all over it. Someone with a whole lot of clout had shut down this case and moved it out of the only capable law enforcement in the state. Agent Thornton was not knocking the local law enforcement per se, it's just that FBI are all trained the same whether you are stationed in Chicago or Tim Buck Too. Locals who may or may not have the same level of expertise on the various crime fighting tactics train local law enforcement agents. The FBI had access to the federal database and the most up to date crime lab in the country, the world perhaps. There was no reason on Earth to move any investigation out of the feds into the local jurisdiction unless you did not want to solve the crime. Someone, with a lot of power, did not want this child found. This case had become political, and he knew that they were letting someone get away with murder.

Robert welcomed the call from Agent Thibodeau. He could feel the weight of this case lifting off his shoulders, as the opportunity to fully investigate would soon be in the hands of the FBI. Tim said that he had enough evidence to reclaim jurisdiction over the case. Tim was a good agent and if he said that they had enough, they had enough. Robert admonished Tim for going out on his own and told him better be sure of his facts. Tim was adamant that he had more than enough. Robert found himself smiling and then realized that this case was almost two years old. Whatever evidence there had been was long gone by now, but Tim said he had what he needed to arrest of Andy Morrell.

CHAPTER FORTY-SIX

Tim stretched his legs out in front of him as far as they could go and laced his finger behind his head. Exhausted beyond belief, Tim was very pleased with him self at the same time and felt like celebrating. *I'll celebrate when the son of bitch Morrell is behind bars.* The thought jolted him back to reality. He had connections and a plausible story of what happened, but he still didn't have any real proof. There is no smoking gun in this case, no body.

What do I know? Tim looked at his notes and reviewed what he knew. I know that Karen was not "dating" Andy. Andy might have thought she was dating him, but not his type. She met him on an online dating site and when she learned that he was to have physical custody over his 2-year-old daughter she flew to Maine to meet him. I know that Karen was working for Lev Odessa out of Long Island, New York. Lev Odessa was part of the notorious, The Odessa Family AKA Russian Mafia. Of course, being related to the family did not make you a crook. The Odessa family and all its dealings were all hypotheticals within the bureau. The family was ruthless and had ways of eliminating any incriminating evidence or witnesses. No one who knew anything would go against the family. The Bureau had an ongoing investigation, last Tim knew they were the most wanted family, but there was nothing solid to even issue a search warrant. *The involvement of the Odessa Family should be more than enough to get this case back into FBI jurisdiction.*

Karen was a glorified secretary. She found the marks and made the appointments, the rest was handled by someone else. She made a mistake to go and meet Andy Morrell in Maine. As far as Tim could tell, Karen never met any of her marks in person, she chatted them up online and agreed to meet in person, but then that was when the others would take over. That is the part where it gets sketchy. Tim did not know if Lev met the target or someone else did. Someone met them and someone took them elsewhere, but who and where was beyond what Karen knew.

Tim realized that he still only really had theory. He had a list of contacts from Karen's computer of missing girls and some of the chat records. A search of the online dating records should give him enough. Tim outlined the basics to his partner Max and asked him to follow up with the online dating sites. He told Max to get all the records between Karen and the list of missing girls so far. Tim was bringing Karen's laptop back with him to have is tech guys go over it and see what they could find. As savvy as Karen was with her online searches, she was not savvy enough to protect her laptop. She must have been convinced, like most criminals, that she was too smart to get caught.

CHAPTER FORTY-SEVEN

*H*abits, *I love habits.* Special Agent Timothy Thibodeau routine was like clockwork. He got up every morning at precisely five AM, you could set your watch on how precise he is, you see the lights go on in the bedroom and yep, it's five AM. Five minutes later he is out in front running down the street. He ran five miles, five point two to be exact, took him one hour door to door. That was the amazing thing, it took him one hour regardless of weather or day. He never bested his time or took longer on his run, it took him an hour and he was back at exactly 6:05 AM everyday. He was on the road to work at 6:30 sharp every morning.

The federal building on Harlow Street took Agent Thibodeau over the Main Street Bridge crossing the Penobscot River. Traffic was nonexistent at that time in the morning. The bridge itself was old and had no shoulder. A simple four-foot high guardrail ran the length. During the winter the bridge was down right treacherous. It would be so easy to cause an accident on the bridge. A simple bump from behind off center could force the car to spin towards the waterside of the bridge, a second bump would send the car over the bridge into the water. The damage would be substantial and there would be no way to determine the cause of the accident. A fall at this height would be fatal no matter what safety features were your car had. Airbags would not help if your frontend smashed into the backseat. The best of all is there would be no witness, no traffic cams to worry about, problem solved. *Habits, they make my life easy.*

CHAPTER FORTY-EIGHT

Tim had to admit that if felt good to be in his own bed. The alarm went off at 5:00 AM and Tim hit the snooze for the first time in his life. Tim mentally reviewed the facts in the case against Andy Morrell. His gut told him that the meeting with Karen was about selling his two-year-old daughter to the Russian Mob. Karen was killed because she screwed up with her "in person meeting". The Russian Mob had ties all over the place, including politicians and police. They were this generation's version of the "Untouchables". *How did they get Al Capone? Income Taxes?* Tim's evidence was shaking on this connection, but he hoped he had enough for an honest judge to issue a search warrant. The biggest link was that shyster law firm. Alone that law firm connected Karen, Andy, The Odessa Family, and Senator Richards. Senator Richards was another major weakness in Tim's facts. He knew she was involved, but he did not know why.

Today was the biggest day in Tim's career. He had gone out on a limb investigating this case. He had gone against a direct order to halt the investigation and he had better be sure he had enough to reopen the investigation. This case was a career maker or breaker, specifically his. A lot of lives and careers were on the line. If the senator was involved then so were a lot of other people up and down the chain of command. *What did they have on the Senator to involve her?*

To distract his line of thinking, Tim turned on the radio, he listened to some spokesperson from the CDC talking about the relative safety of treating the first Ebola case in the US. *Never before had there been a case of Ebola in the US, and now the CDC was bringing one in.* "The disease, albeit lethal, is very difficult to contract. In order to contract the disease one must be in direct contact with bodily fluids," the CDC spokesperson was saying. *If it is so hard to contract then how did the doctor contract the disease? You would think that a doctor, of all people, would know better and never break protocol with this deadly disease.* Lost in his thoughts about the brewing catastrophe of introducing Ebola into this country, he did not notice the approaching suburban. The suburban barreled down on the government issue Ford making full contact with a bumper. Tim looked in his rearview mirror and saw the black suburban. "What the Fuck!" Tim swore turning around trying to maintain control of his car. The suburban kept pushing his car. Tim had nowhere to go, he applied the brake, but the suburban kept pushing him onto the bridge.

Tim laid on the horn screaming at the driver. "Back the fuck off!" Tim applied the brake with both feet, but the suburban continued to push his car. The Suburban turned sharply to the left to break away, but that maneuver sent Tim's government issue Ford into a clockwise spin towards the edge of the bridge. There was nothing Tim could do to prevent his car from careening off the bridge. Time slowed to a crawl as Tim watched the guardrail of the bridge approach the car. His car went through the guardrail as if it were paper. He could feel the G-force as he went over the bridge, like being in a roller coaster. Tim's mind went blank. His life did not flash before him as he plunged to his death. Tim watch in frozen horror as his death approached. He heard the impact of the front end of his car with the water and then everything went black.

CHAPTER FORTY-NINE

"**W**hat do you know of the new girl?" Sally starts immediately.

Still groggy with sleep, Casey replies, "I like her. She is a hard worker and does best when she is working with others. When she works alone she goes to this other spot and she is really angry. You can feel her hostility half way across the room. You can see the other kids in the class give her a lot of space when she gets like this."

"Yeah, I tried to get her to open up with me yesterday, but she said she was fine. I asked about her living situation and did not have much to say about that."

"Same with me, she is great until the topic gets personal and she clams up."

Sally stared out her window thinking about the new girl. *I love autumn in Maine.*

Casey hated to be up this early in the morning. First she was missing her breakfast with her daughter and second, she like to sleep. She had forgotten what good sleep felt like for so long when she was on the run, but now that she is sure she is safe, sleep was one of the best things in the world. *What is the big deal about this new girl that I had to come in early to talk about her?* It wasn't like Sally to call early morning meeting to discuss a student. Something was up here.

"Sally, why don't you just tell me what is on your mind and maybe I can help." Casey said to Sally's back.

The crack of the window followed by the hiss of air sent an alarm up Casey's spinal cord. She felt the recognition like a blow to her head. Terror seized Casey as she watched frozen in place. Sally fell back falling over the arm of her chair dropping the coffee cup on her way. Casey stared at the round blood spot on Sally's forehead.

Casey's mind turned to a different time in her life and all she could see were dead bodies strewed about the streets. The rising panic in her threatens to take control. She had been so certain that she was out of harm's way here, that she was safe. The face of the man she loved floated into her vision and she pushed the thoughts away. *Oh God, what about Georgia? What about Tom? Oh my God! They found me.*

CHAPTER FIFTY

Casey moved to the window approaching from the side ducked below the line of sight. Peering over out the corner of the window she saw the unmistakable flash of light from a riflescope. The flash came from the top window of the Moose Pub Cafe. *Oh Shit! Oh Shit! Oh Shit! Get a grip! Think! What do I do?*

Taking a deep breath Casey forced herself to look out the window towards the Moose Pub Café. She saw the man slip out from around the back of the pub and cross the street. The man was in a hurry, but not running, a professional and carrying a rifle case. *Think Casey Think! I should call the police, but then I will have to give a statement. Oh God, I can't. I have to get out of her now. I have to get to Tom and Georgia. Oh God! Tom and Georgia! I have to get to them. Think. Okay. Leave now!*

Casey looked at her friend on the floor and said a silent prayer for her safe journey to the next world. "I'm sorry dear friend." It was still early and no one else had arrived at school yet. Casey still had time to get out of there before anyone knew she had been there. Casey left the office quickly and slipped out the back door away from the one security camera. She skirted the tennis court making a large arc to avoid being caught on camera and went to her car. Checking the time she sighed relief knowing that the camera would not be turned on for another 6 minutes. She started the car and drove to her house. She drove past her house and turned down the neighbor's driveway and parked. The neighbors were part-timers and she knew no one was home. She had a good view of her house and everything looked normal. She could see Tom sitting at the kitchen island with his coffee checking something out on his tablet.

Tom looked up when she entered the door and smiled. "Now what did you forget?" He laughed.

Casey shook her head and put her fingers to her lip to indicate for him to be quiet. She went to the phone and called the school's secretary.

"Hello?"

"Marla, hi, it's Casey. I don't feel so well, I think I caught a bug or something. Can you get me a sub?

"Will do, you feel better."

"Oh, Marla, I was supposed to meet with Sally this morning can you let her know I am out sick today?"

"No problem. Are you okay? You don't sound good."

"No, I am in a bad way, but I'll be fine. Thanks, Marla. Thanks for everything."

Tom was staring at Casey, "What was that all about?"

"Sally's dead. They found me."

"We have to go."

"No shit."

Tom moved to the basement and brought up the two suitcases that were already packed ready to make a quick getaway. He looked at Casey and his eyes betrayed fear. Casey heart leaped into her throat and she could feel the heat of guilt make her face red. The moment passed and Tom shook his head and mouthed, "We're going to be fine." Tom turned and became all business and headed for the door.

"Let's get a move on." Tom yelled from the doorway heading out to the garage.

"Okay, I have to pack a bag for Georgia." Casey threw clothing, diapers, and supplies in a large gym bag. *Extra shoes, coats... What am I forgetting? I should have had this prepared. Stupid Stupid Woman!" That will have to do.*

Casey grabbed a briefcase and the gym bag and placed

them by the front door. She went upstairs to wake her daughter and dress her.

"Got to go sweetheart, you can sleep in the car."

Thirty-five minutes later Casey, Georgia, and Tom were heading out of town in their VW Toureg. *Don't look back its bad luck... Don't look back.*

CHAPTER FIFTY-ONE

Tom wanted to step on the gas and get the hell out of there. It had been so long since they were on the run and it was before Georgia. Tom held back his urge to flee in a frenzy. He turned right out of the driveway and followed the road to the main highway leading out of town. Left took him to Bangor and Right took him north to Canada. Tom headed north. *Let's put an international boarder between us.* Tom looked over at Casey, but she was staring out the window. Tom reached over and held her hand. Casey turned at his touch to look at him.

"I am so sorry." Casey whispered.

"Nothing to be sorry about. I knew what I signed on for a long time ago." Tom's voice was reassuring.

Casey looked at her daughter in the back seat. Georgia was sound asleep, she looked just like an angel when she slept. From the first moment I saw her sleeping, I thought she looked like an angel.

"North? Canada?" Casey asked.

"I'm thinking lets put an international boarder between us." Tom smiled.

It was still early by the town's standards, very few people were out and about as they headed north. They pass by the local gas station and some of the regulars were just starting to show up. Tom nodded and waved to his neighbors as they past. Casey ducked down in her seat so no one would notice her in the car. In this town, everyone waved to everyone and everyone knew everyone's business. If she called in sick and was seen driving out of town with Tom, that would be big gossip.

They past a green Suburban with damaged to passenger's frontend. Tom did not know the car or the driver. Tom did not like the idea of a stranger in town considering. No reason for strangers to be around this time of year. The driver just stared at Tom as they drove past one another, giving Tom a chill. Tom watched his rearview mirror to see if the green Suburban would turn around, but it didn't. *Must have imagined the guy was staring at me. The damage to the frontend was odd, not something you would see if the guy hit an animal. If he hit an animal you would expect damage up on the hood.*

They traveled out of town north. As soon as they were 5 miles out of town they were the only ones on the road. Tom continued to check the rearview mirror to make sure there was no sign of anyone, especially that green Suburban.

"You can sit up now" Tom said.

"Thank you, I was starting to get a cramp." Casey looked around massaging her thigh, her shoulders were all tense from anxiety. She was scared. "I really thought we were okay." She shook her head as tears filled her eyes threatening a full breakdown.

"Keep it together Casey we have a lot of work to do." Tom was stern, but reassuring. "I'm thinking Quebec City, the Old Port."

The road was rough and in need of repair forcing them to keep the car under 50 mph the whole way. Casey was surprised that Georgia could sleep through the bumpy ride, but of course this is all she ever knew. *I'm so sorry to have to tear you away from everything you have ever known.*

CHAPTER FIFTY-TWO

C hief Sanders had just walked into his office when the phone started ringing. He debated whether to answer it or just let the caller call back later. Sighing, he grabbed the receiver, "Redwood Police, Chief Sanders speaking."

"Hey Jeff, there's been an accident over at the school. I think Sally is dead."

Jeff could hear Marla from the school say, but he was having trouble getting his head around it.

"Say again."

"Just get over here, it's bad." Marla hung up the phone.

Jeff stood holding the dead phone for a moment soaking in what he heard. Grabbing the keys to his squad off the desk, Chief Sanders took off for the school.

Jeff pulled up to the school's front door with his red lights going and noticed students milling about outside. It was just before 8 o'clock and the first bell was due to ring in 5 minutes.

"Christ!" Chief Sanders exclaimed seeing all the students he realized that no one had bothered to cancel school. Walking into the building he bellowed at Marla, "Get these kids out of here! This is a crime scene for crying out loud." Walking into Sally's office he stopped in his tracks, taking in the whole scene.

Sally's body was laying face up with an entry wound dead center of her forehead. This was not the first unfortunate hunting accident Jeff had scene, but this was the first time that the victim was a personal friend and not another hunter. Hunting accidents like this were more common than most people thought, at least one hunter was accidently shot to death by his buddy each season, but usually inexperience and alcohol played a part in that. It was unusual to have an accident like this in town, this early in the morning.

"Who found her?" Jeff asked to anyone listening.

"I did." Marla walked up behind Jeff.

Jeff looked around the office. "Anyone hear the shot?"

"As far as I know, she was alone. Casey called me this morning and said she had a meeting with her, but she's sick and asked me to tell Sally… it's the reason I came down here."

Jeff frowned as he looked at the second mug of half finished coffee on the bookshelf by the door. Walking over he picked the cup up and smelled the coffee. It was cold, but the coffee smelled fresh.

"What about the second cup of coffee?" Jeff held up the Bates coffee mug.

Shrugging her shoulders not thinking much of the cup of coffee Marla said, " that cup could be a week old, Sally always has multiple cups of coffee going, she's kind of absent mined like that. Was absent minded…" Marla's voice trailed off as the enormity that her friend and colleague was dead.

"Marla," Jeff said gently. "Call whoever you need to and close the school down and send everyone home. No one needs to be here as we process this scene."

Marla nodded her tear stained face and wen to make the calls.

What a waste. Jeff thought to himself.

CHAPTER FIFTY-THREE

Approaching the boarder, Tom looked over at Casey.

Reading his mind, Casey said, "better use our real IDs, all the border guys know us. We'll change them up when we get to the hotel"

Casey stared out the window as they made their way to the border. It was a ten-mile trek between the boarder town and the actual border. *I thought we were safe. I never would have considered having Georgia if I thought we were still in danger. Why send someone to kill me? What good am I to them dead?*

Georgia continued to sleep in her car seat. She looked so peaceful and content, oblivious of the danger they were in. *I'm so sorry, I thought we were safe,* Casey sends a silent prayer to whoever might be listening to her.

"Hey Casey, hey Tom. I heard on the radio that school was canceled? What's up with that?" Bruce asked Casey while glancing at their paperwork. Bruce had been one of the first friends they made up here. He worked the boarder, but lived in Redwood. He said he loved the lake too much to live away from it.

"Not really sure." Casey tried to hide her surprise. "Just got a call that school was closed so we thought we make a day trip to St. George." Casey hoped she was believable.

"Should have good weather for it. Have fun." Bruce handed back their paperwork and waved them on.

Trying to see if Bruce knew anything more, Casey leaned over Tom and asked, "Hey Bruce? Had much traffic in the last couple of days?"

"Not much, just same old log trucks. Not really a big tourist time."

Tom gave Casey a look that said to shut-up and said, "well, always good to see you, Bruce, but we better get going if we want to enjoy the day."

"Have a good one, see you later."

Tom pulled away from the boarder crossing and shot another look at Casey.

"What?" Casey asked.

"What are you doing?"

"Just trying to get information."

"Keep in mind, Bruce thinks we are on a day trip and nothing more."

Casey realized that Tom was right. Not like Bruce would know if a hit man crossed the boarder. "Sorry, Tom. I'll start using my head."

"You better, this is really serious Casey. You need to have all your wits about you."

Casey felt the weight of the world on her shoulders and they continued their trip to Quebec City in silence.

CHAPTER FIFTY-FOUR

Tom, Casey, and Georgia stop at a roadside café on the outskirts of St. George for a breakfast. Tom and Casey ate there whenever they traveled this way the food was excellent and cheap. Walking inside, Casey realized that they had not been here since before Georgia was born. The place was exactly as Casey remembered and this brought a sense of relief, inhaling deeply Casey smelled all the same sumptuous smells.

The waitress, Claudette, immediately recognized them, but was surprised by Georgia. Casey smiled and introduced her daughter in broken French. She immediately held Georgia up in her arms and started gushing pleasantries over the little girl. Georgia instantly took a liking to the waitress and giggled and smiled at ever word uttered. Claudette brought crayons and paper for Georgia to draw on while we decided what to order. Casey did not realize how hungry she was until she started to read the menu.

"I'm starved, I could eat one of everything." Tom laughed.

"My sentiments exactly." Casey said starting to relax.

Looking over the menu she decided on the Shepard's Pie for herself and grilled chicken for Georgia. Tom ordered baked haddock with all the sides. There was no telling when they would get a meal this good again in the foreseeable future.

"I say we stay in Quebec City for a while. Make it our base while we figure things out." Casey stated while they waited for their meal. In the past, before Georgia, spending the weekend in Quebec City was a real treat. "We have to assume that they know the names we are using and we will have to pick different IDs once we get there."

Tom liked the idea of staying in Quebec City for a few days. "Agreed." Tom smiled for the first time since the drama unfurled earlier this morning. "We can stay at that cute B & B just outside of the city's center. The one we always wanted to stay at. That way we can use our new IDs without arousing suspicion. This time of year the place should be all, but deserted. We might even have the place to ourselves."

"Sounds perfect." Casey began to relax as details of the next steps were ironed out. Both Tom and Casey ate and played with Georgia at the table as if nothing had happened. The sweet gales of laughter coming from the child attracted smiles from the other patrons in the café. Laughter is a universal language. The pure unadulterated joy of the young and innocent could sweep away even the most harden scrooge.

Tom, Casey, and Georgia reached the B & B with the spirit of a well-deserved holiday. As they had hoped, the place was empty of guest and only one reservation for the weekend. They inquired about the possibility of staying at the Inn an extended time and the Inn Keeper replied that they could stay as long as they wanted. "What do I care if I rent to you or someone else, a bird in the hand and so forth." The Inn Keeper mumbled as she showed them to a two-room suite on the top floor. "The stairs are a bugger, but this is the best view in the whole place."

Casey looked out the window and agreed that being on the top floor was well worth the stairs. This gave them the advantage of being able to see anyone approaching the Inn and privacy because there were no other rooms on the top floor. "It's perfect."

The two rooms bedrooms each had their own bath and were joined with a parlor. The parlor had a working fireplace on the interior side of the room and a long window seat on the other side of the room. The view looked over the old city and St. Lawrence waterway. The view was nothing less than spectacular. The room was decorated with a couple of overstuffed armchairs, an upholstered couch, and tray coffee table. Casey carried the bags into a large bedroom with a king size bed and told Tom she was going to go down and settle up with the owner.

Georgia was running about the place opening up drawer and exploring everything. She clearly liked it here. Tom smiled and watched his daughter explore. The reason being lousy it was still nice to have this adventure with his daughter. This is a magical city, and they really should have brought Georgia here before now.

The built in cabinet next to the fireplace contained a TV. Tom turned it on and started searching for world news. The TV stations were split between French and English stations, but Tom was having trouble finding the Canadian equivalent to CNN or any local news station. Tom was going through the station when he landed on the cartoon station. The musical refrain for Sponge Bob caught Georgia's attention and she pleaded to watch. The station was in French, but Georgia did not seem to care, cartoons were cartoons in any language. Maybe if they stay here long enough Georgia will learn French.

Casey returned from downstairs to find Georgia sitting on the floor watching Sponge Bob in French. She immediately started to chuckle, the whole world could change and some things never change. Tom came up behind her and wrapped her in his arms. Casey pressed up against Tom's body allowing her to feel his strength and security.

"We need to talk about all this and come up with a plan." Tom started.

"I know, but for right now, can we just be?" Casey murmured leaning on Tom and watching the characters speak French and hearing her daughter giggles as if she understood the joke.

CHAPTER FIFTY-FIVE

The first light of morning came streaming into the bedroom. Casey was curled up next to her daughter with her husband on the other side. They all fit quite well on the king size bed. The mattress was exceptionally comfortable and the down comforter made everything so plush and decadent. *This is the best sleep I have had in a long time.* Casey untangled her arms from her daughter and slipped out of bed in search of the bathroom.

The bathroom was a traditional four-piece bathroom with a separate tub and shower, pedestal sink, and toilet. The fixtures and tile were all in white, white towels, white ceramic on chrome faucets. The room was cold and sterile compared to the warmth and coziness of the bedroom. Casey liked it; she never was big on luxurious bathroom. Bathrooms are functional rooms with a solitary purpose. Casey quickly used the bathroom and returned to bed slipping between the warm sheets and assuming her position snuggled up next to her daughter. She was wide-awake and closed her eyes for a second and promptly fell right back to sleep. This time the dreams were anything, but sweet.

Casey heard the explosion and started to run in the direction of the smoke. Everyone else was running away. She could see the bodies strewed about the streets and sidewalks. Old women were kneeling and wailing out sorrow for their lost loved ones. Casey did not know what to do. She was searching for Ana, but she could not find her. She started to scream out Ana's name, but no sound came out of her mouth. She had no voice. Two men grabbed her by the arms on both sides and shoved her into a waiting car. She tried to get away and find Ana, pleading with her captors that she needed to find her daughter, but they were silent on both sides of her as the car sped out of town towards the mountains. Casey looked out the back window at the retreating scene crying for her daughter.

CHAPTER FIFTY-SIX

C asey could till hear the explosion behind her. A series of explosions from right to left one after another Boom da boom da boom. She could feel the shockwave on her back and immediately crouched to the ground covering her head with her arms. She could hear the screaming, wailing, running, pandemonium breaking out behind her. She did not want to move. She did not want to turn around. She was afraid of what she would see. She had seen it all before, smelled it all before, and heard it all before.

"Wake up Mama!" Georgia held her mother's face between her little hands.

"Casey, you're okay. Wake up. You're dreaming. Wake up!" Casey could hear Tom saying through the fog of sleep. Tom was gently shaking Casey trying to wake her up.

Casey opened her eyes wide and saw her daughter's face inches from her own. "I'm sorry sweetie. I was having a nightmare."

"About monsters?" Her daughter asked.

"I don't remember." The content of the dreams faded immediately on waking up, but the intense sense of fear lingered. And the pain of losing Ana all over again as if it had just happened, that was how this all started they killed Ana trying to get to me.

"I have to go back. I have to fix this once and for all. I need to know what is going on." Casey said out loud.

"I know. I'll start packing." Tom started to get out of bed.

"No, you and Georgia have to stay here. I need to do this, alone and I *need* to know that you two are safe."

"I can't let you do this alone."

"You have to, you have to take care of Georgia. Promise me you will take care of Georgia." Casey pleaded.

"You know I will." Tom hugged both his wife and child in a hug that will have to last them a long time.

CHAPTER FIFTY-SEVEN

Tom pulls into their driveway and stops. "I really don't want to see the house right now."

"I understand. I love you and will join you shortly. Until I know what is going on don't expect me to call. Remember no news is good news." Georgia is fast asleep in the back. Casey kisses Tom and jumps out of the car. She opens the back car door, leans in, and kisses her daughter. "I love you sweetie."

"I love you too," Georgia says in her sleep.

Casey walks down the driveway without looking back. She hears Tom pull out of the driveway. Tears begin to pour down her face with the threat of overwhelming her, *I'm going to makes this right.* She tells herself. *Looking on the bright side, at least now I have my car.*

Nothing appears to be out of place as Casey approaches the house. She quietly opens the passenger side door of her Audi Q5 and reaches under the front seat. Her gun is right where she left it. Casey can barely remember when she did not travel with a loaded gun in her car. Being a teacher, and a Quaker, everyone assumed Casey was a die-hard liberal anti-gun type. Casey did nothing to dissuade them of this notion. *The less people know, the better I am.* Sometimes the only advantage you have is the one of surprise.

Holding the gun, Casey approached the house peering in through the windows before entering, she did not see anyone or anything that looked out of place. She entered the house from the front door and stood in the entryway. This house was beautiful. The front entryway was grandiose with ceilings that soared almost thirty feet. The front half of the house was open floor from the kitchen to the living space. A huge stone fireplace was on the exterior wall framed by two sets of French doors. From the front door, Casey could see the entire expanse of the room and up into the loft area. Clear. She moved down the hall to the looking into the pantry on her right, no one there, and continued down the hall to the master bedroom. The door was open, and no one was there, stepping into the room she checked the walk-in closet to her right. No one. She moved into the master bath on the left and continued through to the laundry room. No one she moved to her left down the hall opening the linen closet on her way, no one. No one in the powder room. She stopped at the top of the basement steps and crouched low to see under the first floor. She crept down the landing. No one anywhere there and nowhere to hide here the basement was unfinished and just an open space from one side of the house to the other. Tom always said the house was well designed and said to prove it you can ride a bicycle around in this house without stopping. Casey relaxed walking down the hall to the front stairs to check the upstairs. She was confident at this point that no one was in the house because what she knew about this house that an intruder would not know is that the vaulted ceilings created a concert hall effect for acoustics. You could whisper upstairs and hear it clear as a bell downstairs. It was a flaw in the house she hated until right at this moment. Regardless, Casey still climbed the stairs to the second floor and made sure no one was hiding. All clear.

Casey made a cup of coffee as she collected her thoughts. The one sadness of her predicament was leaving this house. This house had been an albatross of work, but it kept them busy and preoccupied. We would never have had Georgia if we did not feel safe. No regrets, having Georgia was the best thing that ever happened to any of them.

For so long after Richard, Casey did not think she would ever be with anyone and then she met Tom. With Tom, her life was pleasant and content until they came looking for her. She didn't even know that she was connected to any of this until they came looking for her. That was when Tom stepped up and got her to safety. He found Redwood, built a house, and created a new life for them. It was a good life. *Damn it!*

Enough of the self-indulgence, Casey chastised herself. I need to figure out what to do. I guess I should start at the beginning. The house was obviously undisturbed suggesting that maybe this was not about her, but she needed to know for sure. If they are not looking for me, what had Sally gotten herself into? Casey called the school and got the recorded greeting she punched in the extension for the Kelly, the Principal.

"Hi, this is Kelly," The school Principal answered on the first ring.

"Hi, it's Casey. I need to come in and talk to you. Are you free today?"

"If you can be here in the next couple of minutes, we could meet that is if a parent does not beat you to me." Kelly laughed.

"I'll be right there."

Casey put her coffee cup down in the sink and left the house. She put her gun back in its case under the front passenger's seat of her car and took off to school. It took her less than five minutes to drive to the school, park her car, and make it to the Principal's office. *I am going to miss working so close to home.*

Casey told Kelly that she needed to take some time off because she was really freaking out about Sally. "I was with her when it happened. I didn't know what to do I was so scared I just ran away." Casey confessed

"I know." Kelly said matter-of-factly.

"What do you mean, *I know?* How?"

"The second coffee cup, in the Bates College mug. You are the only one who meets with Sally before school, and you always drink out of the Bates College mug."

Casey was impressed she didn't think Kelly was so aware of her surroundings. She laughed, "my bad for thinking I could put one over you."

"Ha, but seriously, Marla said that Jeff Sanders noticed the second coffee cup."

"Well, whatever, it's not like I could add to the investigation. I heard they ruled it a hunting accident?"

"That's what they say, but so far no hunters have come forward saying they were in the area."

"Well, I will only need a few days and I will come in at night and get my work done. I just can't deal with being around students right now.

"Take all the time you need. I know you two were close."

"Thanks, I really appreciate this."

Casey return to her house feeling optimistic for the first time since the running began. She had a partial plan shaping up.. Casey had a master key for the school, all the teachers had one. Of course, the expectation was that you only use it to open your classroom, but it came in handy sometimes when you needed to get something out of someone else's classroom. It was really handy when you forgot your keys at home and any teacher in the building could open your room. *Now she would use it to spy on Sally. If I go in really late even the custodial staff will have gone home. Then I can get a look at what Sally was working on, whom she called, and hopefully and hopefully...* Casey did not finish the thought. She would just have to wait and see. *I could use a little help here.* Casey sent a prayer to her friend.

CHAPTER FIFTY-EIGHT

C asey sat in Sally's chair facing her computer screen. The screen requires a username and password. The username was easy, it's her e-mail address like every staff member in the school. The password was another thing. The school required a combination of letters, numbers, and symbols for security.

Sally was like Casey and would never remember such a complicated password and Casey hoped that the password was saved somewhere near her computer, but so far no such luck. Where would I keep the password if it were me? *If it were me?... I would have the password on a sticky note within reach of the computer within my line of sight.* Sally looked to her right and there on the bookcase were a bunch of sticky notes with phone numbers and reminders. In the middle of the sticky notes was one note that read $chool14. That was the original password, *Sally had never changed her password.*

In no time at all, Casey was able to access Sally's phone records. Sally's computer automatically tracked every call that she made, but the details of the call had to be entered manually. It appeared Sally was pretty good about adding names and even some details about the call. *Wow, she talked to tons of people every day.* Most of the names Sally recognized, but one name in particular jumped out at her. *Tim T FBI, that has to be what I am looking for.* Casey knew that Sally had a childhood sweetheart who grew up to be a G-Man. It was a source of pride that Sally knew an actual FBI agent. *This must be him.* Casey wrote down the number deciding to call him first.

Casey stared at all the other numbers wondering what, if anything, they might mean. She was thinking about her last conversation about the new girl. The conversation was a bit odd and it was weird that Sally had asked her to come to an early morning meeting. Just thinking about that morning brought tears to her eyes and the rise of emotions that threatened to overwhelm her. Casey's eyes drifted over the computer screen and she noticed a podcast icon.. Casey clicked on the podcast and discovered that Sally recorded every meeting she had in her office, staff, students, anyone. Casey first reaction was a sense of betrayal that her friend had recorded their conversations without telling her, but instantly forgave her friend understanding that these days with allegations a person had to do what a person had to do. There were too many recordings so Casey decided to e-mail the folder to herself and listen to them at the house. Casey had a second thought to e-mail the phone log for the past month as well.

Given the size of these files, it will take a while to upload and e-mail them. Casey went up to her classroom to write lesson plans for the week. On her way out of the building, Casey checked Sally's office and noticed the e-mail had successfully sent their messages. Casey clicked on the history and deleted the parts of the history that included her searches. Deleting partial histories never raised any suspicions, but some people make the mistake of clearing the entire history and that always grabs the attention to anyone who is looking. She logged out of Sally's computer and went home. I can always come back if I need anything else.

The thought of going back to the house all alone brings on a profound sorrow as a knot rises in her throat, she thinks, *no Tom no Georgia*. Casey is so mad that this is happening to her again, but what can she do? She has to figure this out. Until now, Casey had never been apart from her daughter for more than a few hours. The idea of being away from her made her chest hurt. From day one, Georgia never liked the crib and slept in bed with Casey. She would fuss and cry anytime you laid her down. Neither Casey nor Tom could stand to see her fuss and would hold her in their arms until she fell asleep. Sometimes, Casey would try to lay Georgia down in her crib after she fell asleep, but Georgia always woke. Georgia could immediately sense any separation and would start fussing again. Even as a newborn in the hospital, Georgia would not sleep in the bassinet provided by the hospital and so started the habit of mother and daughter sleeping side by side. *I thought for sure she would grow out of it,* but even three years later, Georgia still only fell asleep with either Tom or Casey laying down right next to her.

Damn it! Why now? The fact that Casey knew that this was not some random hunting accident, it was cold-blooded murder, put her whole world in jeopardy. Thinking about how calm the guy was walking away from the pub sent shivers down her spine, *this guy was a professional.* What she needed to figure out is whether the hit was on Sally or was it for her. *That guy was too much of a professional to make that kind of mistake. We were in Sally's office not mine and there is little reason to believe the hit man knew I was in the room. He wouldn't have left me as a witness.*

Feeling a little sense of relief that maybe this was not about her, Casey felt impatient to figure this out and get back to Tom and Georgia and her life. With that thought blasting in her head, Casey was eager to start listening to the office recordings of her friend and colleague. Casey was confident that somewhere in all that mess she would find the answer.

CHAPTER FIFTY-NINE

Casey was too wired to get any sleep so she set up the stereo system to listen to Sally's recordings. A month's worth of recordings and so far nothing. Casey was right where she started. Casey stood up and stretched this is like, *what is that expression? Watching paint dry.* Casey fought the impulse to jump ahead. She did not want to miss something that could help her. *My whole life is depending on this.*

The constant barrage of complaining that she heard put a new spin on how Casey saw her friend. Wondering how she could put up with so much negativity on a daily basis was astounding and yet Sally always seemed so upbeat and energetic. *All this whining and complaining would drive me to distraction,* Casey thought. How on Earth did she manage to listen to so much crap day in and day out without going postal? Listening to these recordings, it felt like everyone that entered that office came in with some urgent complaint for Sally to fix, including Casey. Casey's mind drifted as she listened to herself whine and complain to Sally. *I never realized how whiny I sounded.* Casey was momentarily distracted and embarrassed about her own behavior. *Nothing like having a mirror put up right in front of you!*

The word *"They sold her..."* drifted into her self-indulgent thoughts. *What?* Casey immediately went to her computer and hit the rewind button. *They sold her.* Casey looked at the label of the podcast, Theresa Rowe. *Who sold who or what? Is she talking about sister? How does Theresa know this?* Casey had hundreds of questions flood her at once. Casey rewinds the conversation to the beginning.

Casey pulse quicken as she listened to the recording, she easily recognized the voice of Theresa Rowe and her friend Sally. Casey feels an almost out of body experience as she listens intently to the conversation.

"You have not turned in a single assignment since you transferred here. How do you expect to pass?" Sally started the conversation.

"Maybe I don't care if I pass."

"How's Mrs. Baker's class going?" *They are talking about me.*

"It's okay." Theresa's voice is flat with no inflection.

"No fights? You seem really angry? How's your mom?" Sally's voice probed. *Too many questions Sally – give her a chance to answer.*

"They sold her." Theresa blurted.

"What are you saying? Who?" Sally questions with genuine surprise.

"Just that. They sold my sister for money." Theresa states matter-of-factly. There is a long pause in the conversation.

"You get that I have to report this. Who are they?" Sally almost whispers to Theresa.

"That father of hers, don't know if mom was in on it. Mom is too busy getting high all the time, but we seemed to have some extra money after it happen, after mom got out of rehab. I told those cops about it, thought it would be all taken care of. Nothing happened." Theresa began to sob, "I hope you report it. I hope they listen to you. I hope they arrest their ass. Then maybe I can get my sister back!" Casey hears what sounds like a chair scrapping the floor and feet running fading away.

"Can you find Theresa Rowe?" Casey hears Sally's voice assuming she is on the phone with the office.

Pause.

"No, she got upset and ran out of my office just see if she is still in the building. Is Kelly in her office?" Pause, Casey can hear the sound of feet fading and the door closing.

The recording continues for a few more minutes, silence.

Casey checks the phone log and just what she expected the call to Tim T - FBI follows this conversation with Theresa. Casey looks at the clock, it's just past three in the morning. *I'll have to call Mr. Tim T – FBI first thing in the morning.* Casey smiles for the first time all night.

CHAPTER SIXTY

C asey skims through the rest of the recordings looking for information on Theresa. She finds another conversation between Sally and Theresa where Sally tells Theresa about calling her friend at the FBI and talking with the Principal.

Using a reverse phonebook, Casey looks up the number that Sally called to speak with her friend and finds that it is a number in the Bangor Office on Harlow Street. Casey decides to go see this Tim guy in person and not get stonewall on the phone. Considering the idea that Sally might have been killed due to a phone call to Mr. Tim T - FBI, she realizes making the same call could have the same results.

The drive to Bangor takes her just shy of two hours. She sees a Dunkin Donuts on her right as she comes into town, a line of cars is forming in the drive thru. *Coffee would be good idea right now*. Casey maneuvers her car in line and waits her turn. She is trying to figure out how she will find Tim at the FBI office without knowing his last name. Waiting for her coffee, she realizes that she has not really thought this part through.

The school buses are going as she drives down Broadway towards the center of town. Casey is always amazed to see the bus stop at every house to pick up students. When she was a kid riding the school bus, there was one stop, and we all walk to that one stop and wait for the school bus. The school bus did not just come to you. If you were late, the bus left without you. The buses did not come back and get you. The drivers did not check to make sure someone was home before they dropped you off. All these rules and regulations and still we cannot seem to keep our children safe.

CHAPTER SIXTY-ONE

The federal building on Harlow Street was easy to both locate and drive directly to, which is not always the case in Maine. Casey followed the public parking signs around the building and parked in the half emptied lot. The lot reminded her of the airport, never a problem getting a parking spot.

She entered the building and looked for some type of directory like you find in medical buildings, to point her in the right direction. There did not seem to be any directories. She hesitantly approached the information desk to ask where to go. *What was I thinking? I could just show up and talk to the FBI...*

"I'm looking for the FBI offices?" Casey asked tentatively.

"Third floor, go through the metal detectors over there and the elevator is down the hall on your right." The middle-aged overweight man said with not much interest.

Casey walked over the metal detectors and saw people taking off their shoes and placing them on the belt. She took off her shoes and placed them on the belt with her pocketbook. She walked through without incident, collected her belongs and starting walking towards the elevators looking for a place to sit and put on her shoes. There was a bench opposite the elevators. Casey sat and wondered what she hoped to gain by this meeting.

Casey rode the elevator up to the third floor in an empty car. Stepping off the elevator, she spotted a glass door with the FBI Emblem. The door was locked, but she could see through the glass and people were working and she knocked. Someone from inside buzzed the door, and Casey pulled the doors open and stepped inside. A middle-aged receptionist sitting at a semicircular desk centered in the entryway greeted Casey. She was the gatekeeper and lucky for Casey she seemed amiable.

"Can I help you?" She said remaining seated at her desk.

"I am looking for an agent named Tim," I asked shrugging my shoulders as a way of admitting I did not know the last name.

"And your name is?"

"Casey Baker."

"One minute, please." The receptionist pushed some buttons on her phone system and spoke into the phone. "A Casey Baker is here to see Special Agent Thibodeau. Thank you." Hanging up the phone, she looks up at me. "Someone will be right out to see you just have a seat over there." She pointed to a section of seats along the wall.

I barely sat down when a man in a blue suit approached me with his hand out introducing himself as Special Agent Max Weiss. "I worked with Tim, care to walk with me?"

I shake his hand and follow behind and he navigates me through the inner sanctions off the office space filled with a series of cubicle workspaces to a small office with a door and ushers me inside to have a seat.

"How do you know Tim?" He asks as soon as he shuts the door.

"I don't. He is a friend of a friend of mine, Sally Thornton. Sally and I work together in Redwood." There is a catch in my voice, "we did work together...Sally was killed the other day."

"What do you mean killed?"

"I'd prefer to share this with Tim if you don't mind."

"Tim is dead, he had a freak car accident and his car went off the Main Street Bridge."

"That was him, I heard about that on the news." Casey looked around and stood up. She didn't know what to do now. Her one link was dead. Sally was dead. Unaware she began to pace and wring her hands.

Max watched her for a few moments realizing that she was distraught, but also she knew something and was conflicted about what to do. Max had to help her.

"Let's start again. I should have told you right away that Tim was dead. I was his partner. Anything you would share with him you can share with me. You said Sally was killed. We were lead to believe that it was a hunting accident. Why do you think otherwise?"

"I was there. I peeked out the window right after it happened. I saw a flash from a riflescope and saw a man exiting the Moose Pub Café carrying a rifle case. This guy was a real pro. He walked away quickly, but not in a way to draw attention to himself. This was no hunting accident. The shot occurred in the middle of town, no respectable hunter would think of hunting in town. First off there is no point. Second it is illegal, a guy could lose his license over something like this. And losing your hunting license to some of these guys is a fate worse than death." It was the first time she had voiced all of this out loud.

Max let out a long deep sigh, "This changes things. One accident maybe, two not likely." Max was thinking about Tim and maybe it was not a freak accident. What are the chances of two best friends dying within days of each other? Max could almost hear Tim's boyish voice taunt that there are no such things as coincidences. Max stood and held out his hand, "come on I want to show you something."

Max lead Casey to the conference room that had all of the inner workings of the Alyssa Rowe case including the diagram of people somehow connected. Casey gasps when she sees Karen and Martin. *Oh my God!*

Max and Casey share notes. Max explained that Tim had just returned from a meeting in Miami with El Guapo and was really excited. He believed he had enough evidence to reopen the case. Casey tries hard not to react to the name El Guapo, but she feels like she is about to pee her pants. She could feel the sweat build in her armpits and the back of her knees.

"Reopen the case?" Casey questioned.

"Technically, the case is not closed, but it has been declassified as a cold case and relegated to the local authorities for investigation. Roughly translating that the official investigation has ceased." Max put his hands in his pockets and waited for Casey to react.

"That's crazy it has barely been two years, if that, since Alyssa went missing. Why would the investigation just stop? Come to think of it why wasn't the dad ever charged? I thought you guys worked cases sometimes for decades? My God, at that rate you guys would never have found the Unabomber or Ted Bundy?" Casey began to rant she could not believe what she heard, but she knew that she had to do next. Looking directly at the photo of El Guapo, she was going to Miami.

CHAPTER SIXTY-TWO

C asey paced back and forth as she anguishes over whether to call Tom and tell him that she was going to fly to Miami. She wants to reassure him that they were all fine, but that they had inadvertently stepped into something that needed to be cleared up. She wanted to tell him this was not about her or the Colombia drug cartel, but about the kidnapping of Alyssa Rowe. She wants to tell her husband that this is all a matter of being in the wrong place at the wrong time, but she had never told him that she was not legally married to him. She started to think about how all of this got started.

I went to Colombia as part of my university studies., my semester abroad. I met Martin at a village celebration. It was love at first sight. We were young and crazy in love with one another. I remember every single moment of my life with Martin. From the moment he reached out and touched my hand to the last time I touched his face. On my twenty-first birthday, he asked me to marry him, and I said yes. Five years later I would be cradling the lifeless body of my baby girl in my arms killing my spirit in ways it has never recovered. The Narco-Trafficantes, Colombian Drug Cartels, tried to kill me. Why did they want to kill me? They wanted to send a message to Martin by killing me. They wanted to send a message to the United States by killing an American. They wanted me dead to hurt the ones that loved me most. Sixty-three people died that day including my three-year old daughter, Ana, when they blew up the DAS, the Security Council for Colombia. They killed me too that day. There was no great message to send to the President of the United States, just a lot of dead innocent Pisanos, hardworking citizens, and my daughter. I had no idea that Martin was related to Pablo Escobar. I had no idea that Tio Pablo, the kind Uncle that was at our wedding and offered to walk me down the aisle was the one and only Pablo Escobar, Jefe to the Medellin Drug Cartel. Martin wanted me to stay and he promised to keep me safe. Our daughter was dead and they wanted me dead too. I had no choice, sixty-three innocent people died because of me, including Ana. I had to disappear. I had to become someone else. My leaving was seen as a betrayal to Martin and abandonment of him and my sacred vows. My abandoning Martin and the death of his Uncle left a hole in the cartel to be filled. Martin step in and became El Guapo and that is the last I ever heard from him.

I had no idea that when they finally killed Escobar, they would come looking for me. They would use me as a pawn to get to Martin. They wanted the money that Escobar hid. They, being both my government and the rival cartels. They, being the Colombian government as well. They, that all powerful they, were after me and I had nowhere to hide. Martin would not forgive me for leaving and would offer no assistance. And so I ran. I met and married Tom, changing my name to his. I told Tom that I had gotten into some trouble with the Colombia Drug Cartel and that they thought I actually knew where Pablo Escobar's money was. Tom thought it was ridiculous, at first. But then they came looking and we had to run. We had been in Maine for over ten years, under the name Baker and it was so quiet. We thought we were safe. We were safe and then this. Just being in the wrong place at the wrong time.

Now, my plan was to get on a plane and go and see him, Martin. How could I tell Tom? How could I tell him that I was going to see my husband? Martin hated that I left, but he would not hurt me. *Would he? So much time had past surely he has moved on with his life, new wife, new family.* I need to find out what that agent found out so I could put an end to this. I need to find out what I have gotten myself into without alerting those looking for me that I am still around. The running has to stop. The fear has to stop. If not for me, then for Tom and Georgia.

CHAPTER SIXTY-THREE

It had been years since Casey was on a plane. Flying commercially is really not a good idea when you are in hiding. Casey was trying to remember the last commercial flight she took and really could not remember. She flew home from Colombia when she left Martin. She was relatively safe for a while until they capture and later killed Escobar. I bet my last commercial flight was to Denver. She had a couple of brothers that lived in Denver. She had not spoken with her family in over fifteen years. Casey reflected back to that time, it was so simple and easy. She had gone to Denver for an educational conference put on by NASA. The conference was held at the prestigious Adams Mark hotel in Denver. Casey laughed to herself when she remembered her dreams of being the next teacher to go into space. NASA was recruiting teachers again to go into space as part of them Science, Technology, Engineering, and Math (STEM) push in education. The conference was an information session for the proposed program. Casey did not even get the chance to participate in the selection process because her world turned upside down.

Casey was pretty sure that another teacher never went into space. Who would have predicted the end to the space shuttle missions, NASA's budget cut to almost extinction, or the collapse of the economy in 2008. I stayed with my brother Tony and his family. My brother Jerry was too much of a screw up to be counted on. Tony had always been my favorite brother. As Casey remembered that time she remembered staying up all night talking with her brother about life and the possibilities. *I felt so close to him that night, so at peace with my relationship with him and my whole family. Growing up I felt confident to do whatever I believed was right no matter how hard because I believed in the strength and support of my family. Then when I actually needed their support they were the first to turn on me. At that moment, I knew that no one in my family supported me, and the joke was on me. No one in my family ever did support me it was all a great big lie.*

Casey's eyes watered as she thought about her brother and family. She had not thought of them in so long. Even with Georgia, she had not considered her family. *They had their chance and they blew it.* Casey shoved her thoughts and feeling down deep as the plane began to make its arrival to Miami. The flight to Miami took just over three hours, and the real question plaguing Casey is how she plans to meet with Martin? *I don't have the luxury of thinking about my family and what they did or didn't do. I need to think about what I am going to do here and now.*

The wheels touched down in sunny Florida with barely a bump, a perfect landing. The butterflies in Casey's stomach felt like they were planning a coup. Reaching into her pocket, she read, *2669 S Bayshore Drive Coconut Grove*, the address to her enemy or is it a lion. Am I walking into the lion's den?

The plane taxis to the gate, stops, and the doors open. Everyone on the plane jumps up and starts taking their belongings out of the overhead storage and start disembarking. Casey remains in her seat and waits for the last passenger to get off before her. Looking around the plane she is the last one on board. The flight attendant is at the front door of the plane staring at her with her hands on her hips tapping her toe. Casey stands and stretches and shrugs her shoulders as a Mea Culpa and grabs her carry on suitcase. She descends the stairs and walks into the terminal. She continues walking right out the front door to the taxi stand. Before she knows it she is riding along the waterfront through the heart of Miami toward Coconut Grove.

The air is hot and muggy, and the back of her T-shirt is sticking to her. She is certain that she has perspiration stains under her arms, but is too worried to check. The cab stops at a high-rise right on the water. The fare is thirty-seven dollar even. Casey hands the driver a fifty and tells him to keep the change. He smiles and wishes her a good day. The cab is off into the street traffic before Casey reaches the front door of the high-rise building. The doorman opens the door for her and she hesitates for a moment. The hesitation is slight, but the doorman notices and moves to grab her bag. She clutches the bag tightly and pulls away from the doorman. She is making a scene and needs to get this under control.

"I'm not staying here, perhaps I can leave this bag with you?" She looks at the doorman.

"You can leave it with the receptionist." He states smartly and points to the front desk.

Casey walks to the front desk and stands before a gorgeous blond in a smart blue pinstripe suit.

"I am here to see Paulo Martin."

"Whom shall I say is calling?" She asks professionally eyeballing her up and down.

Pulling herself up straight and tall Casey states, 'Tell him his wife is here." Her confidence belies her terror.

CHAPTER SIXTY-FOUR

T he receptionist picks up the phone and dials a number without taking her eyes off Casey. She repeats what Casey said into the phone with a slight smirk on her face and waits. Her attitude and tone does a one eighty as she points to a bank of elevators. "Take that elevator to the Penthouse." She nods in affirmation.

Casey thanks her and heads to the bank of elevators with her suitcase in tow. She forgot to ask if she could leave it with the receptionist. The elevator hurtles itself towards the top floor like the rocket. Within minutes, the door opens into a huge expanse of white marble. On the perimeter of the room is a wall of windows with the most incredible view of the Gulf of Mexico. Casey reacts to the view with a sharp intake of breath before she can stop herself. She is working hard to remain in control and unafraid.

"It's breathtaking, I know. I think that the day this view doesn't get a reaction from me is the day that I move." Casey hears the old familiar voice.

A lump of sadness rises in Casey's throat threatening to make her bawl. Martin had been her best friend, her one true love. Truth be told Martin was the love of her life. Casey was kidding herself in thinking she could find that kind of love again with Tom, but it was never anything like this. She turned towards the voice and smiled. Casey's whole body shuddered at the sight of him.

Casey responded breathlessly, "absolutely breathtaking" referring to Paulo Martin and not the view. Casey could feel the attraction as if it had only been yesterday. Martin had not changed a bit, except to become even sexier than she remembered.

"I don't know whether to sweep you off your feet and make mad passionate love to you or shoot you." He said sarcastically.

"I vote for neither." Casey attempted at humor. "I am an old tired bitch these days. I see life has treated you well, me not so well." Casey turned to look at the view to quell the sense of unease she felt. Humor has always been her coping defense.

"That is not entirely true from what I've heard. Why are you here?"

"Special Agent Thibodeau is dead and we think it has to do with your sister and what he found out here."

"Quit the bullshit Cassandra!" Martin rolled his r in her full name. No one called her Cassandra distracting Casey track of thought. "What do you mean he's dead? Tell me what you know, right now." Martin stated showing his anger, bringing Casey back to the conversation. It was clear that this was news of the agents death was news to Martin.

"I know about your sister and her involvement with a man name Andy Morrell." Casey started.

"And" Martin demanded.

"Somehow she is connected with him and the disappearance of his little girl named Alyssa Rowe. I know that Special Agent Timothy Thibodeau" emphasizing the full name of the agent, "came down here and met with you and found something out. Officially, the bureau is calling Special Agent Thibodeau's death an accident. I don't buy it. I believe he was killed. I know that Tim was a good friend of my friend Sally Thornton and that Sally was murdered. I know prior to Sally's death she shared a theory that Alyssa Rowe, Andy's kid, had been sold on the black market. That conversation pissed off some seriously badass people leading to her death. That whatever

Agent Thibodeau found out got him killed too. And somehow I am caught dead center of something that could get me and my family killed." Casey paused after her rant and then looked at Martin and sarcastically asked, "Sound about right?" Casey said getting pissed off herself. "What I don't know is what your sister has to do with any of this! I don't know what Agent Thibodeau found out here. Care to enlighten me?" Unable to hide the snarkiness in her voice.

"My sister Karen is dead." Martin said quietly no longer sounding angry, but sad. "I let your Mr. Thibodeau have access to her apartment with the promise he would make those responsible pay."

Casey was taken aback at the news of his sister, her sister. "Martin, I am so sorry to hear about Karen." Casey words seemed so pitiful and empty. Casey turned to face the Gulf of Mexico. "What do I do now? I need to know what is going on. Who is behind it and how to make it go away." Casey said to the view more than to anyone else.

"Mani Venga Aqui (Come Here)" Martin called out. A big man in a muscle shirt entered the room silently and waited. "Tell her what that FBI agent found out."

"He discovered that Senator Jane Richards was involved. Her attorney and Karen's attorney were the same as Andy's attorney. All of the legal bills were paid for by the Senator. Personally." Mani added.

"Why?" Casey asked.

"The agent thought they were blackmailing the Senator, but he didn't find anything that told him what they had on her." Mani stated matter-of-factly, almost militantly.

"And you know all of this, how?" Casey asked.

"Never left the agent's side, part of the deal him having access to Karen's apartment and all."

"Can I check out her home?" Casey turned and asked Martin.

Martin nodded yes and waved her out of there. Mani moved to escort Casey to the elevator. "Mani will take you. I trust you to do what is right. Good-bye."

"Wait we're not done here."

"What more do you want from me?" Martin asked.

"I need to know that this is over between us. That I am safe." Casey pleaded wriggling free of Mani grip.

"Over? Are you kidding? We barely even got started. We never grieved our daughter. You left me." Martin shook his head. "You know what? You do what you have to do. I can't deal with you right now. We'll see when this is all over." Martin waved and turned his back on her ending the conversation completely.

Casey turned on her heels and went with Mani down the elevator and out of the building to a waiting car.

Martin collapsed into a nearby chair. *God almighty help me. I want her back so bad.* Martin sunk deep into the chair letting all the old familiar feelings consume him.

CHAPTER SIXTY-FIVE

Karen Tanneger, Martin's sister, lived in quiet gated condo community of Coconut Grove. Casey thought the small condo community was one of those active adult communities and wondered how Karen ended up living here.

The condo was a lower southern unit of a four unit building with Spanish style architecture. The building complex was nice, but nothing special, nothing to the level of where Martin lived. The cars in the parking lot were all mid-level cost cars. Nothing to suggest an extravagant "party girl" lifestyle, which surprised Casey. Given the fact that Karen was involved in the case, Casey expected glamour and glitz, this place suggested sweet and ordinary.

Mani opened the car door for her and walked her to Karen's unit. He had a key and opened the door and keyed in a code on the security pad. Once inside Mani waited by the front door.

Casey walked around the condo taking it all in. This place did not match the girl she was interested in and wondered why. She looked over at Mani with a questioning look and he just shrugged his shoulders. Her companion, did not care to shed any light on this subject. The unit was a two bedroom with partial views of the beach and water. One of the bedrooms had been converted to an office. Casey sat down at the computer and looked around the desk. *What kind of work did Karen do at this desk?* Casey could not imagine Karen working any kind of job for a living. And yet sitting at the computer in this makeshift office, that was exactly the impression she was getting.

Casey turned on the computer the screen prompted her to enter a username and password. Casey got up and asked Mani if he knew and he said he thought Karen kept all her passwords close at hand. Like the rest of us, Karen was over burdened with having to remember too many passwords. Casey opened the top desk drawer and fount it to be neat and organized a couple of paperclips, a small hand stapler, some pens and pencils, a small wire bound notepad well worn. Casey picked up the notepad and flipped it open. Bingo, it was a list of Karen's username and passwords. She saw the word *KarenT* with the word *birthday* written next to it.

"What's Karen's birthdate?"

Mani replied, "July 15, 1982."

Casey typed in *KarenT and 071582* into the computer. The computer booted instantly bringing Casey to the main windows screen. Casey spotted a desktop folder marked journal and clicked it on. Picking a file at random Casey began to read, *Holy Mother of God, pay dirt!* Casey turned to Mani, "tell your boss I am moving in for the next few days and ask him to have some of his guys secure this place." Casey continued reading hardly believing what she was reading.

Casey searched the journals for a time before the Alyssa Rowe kidnapping. Andy Morrell did not just happen to meet Karen. Karen sought him out. Karen has been hunting people, girls to be specific. Karen has been working directly with a contact named LEV. Karen was a broker of human flesh.

Casey picked up the phone and dialed Max's direct line.

"Special Agent Maxwell Weiss"

"It's Casey, how do we use personal journals as evidence?"

"Bring in the originals."

"What if they are on the computer?"

"E-mail a copy to protect the record and bring in the computer. Our tech guys can authenticate it. Why what gives?"

"I'll tell you when I see you, but first I need to continue working down here." Casey hung up the phone without saying good-bye.

Casey settled in to read Karen's journals knowing that somewhere in these pages were the answers to why a beautiful little girl is missing and why so many people involved have been murdered. Casey printed off several pages of Karen's journal and curled up on the couch to read. Casey was more comfortable holding the print in her hand as she delved into the more intimate life of her one time sister, Karen. Pausing to reflect, Karen had been just a kid when Casey was with Martin. She never knew the adult Karen, who she became and now she was about to get a crash course. Biting down on the end of a pencil Casey started to read.

Karen wrote with exceptional prose that was spellbinding.to Casey. Before she knew it half the night had gone by and she was still tucked up on the couch reading the life and times of Karen Tanneger.

Casey got up to stretch her muscles and to think. But Karen is dead. Casey learned so much about Karen's life and deepest desires to save children from parents that she deemed unfit to raise children. Her contact LEV continued to elude identification and Casey realized that she would have to go and see Martin to ask about this. The last thing she wanted was to face him again. *God help her, she was still in love with him despite everything.*

As if reading her thoughts the door to the condo opened and in walked Martin. He looked so fresh and alert *and stunning.* The surprise of seeing him rendered Casey mute.

"I see we are making ourselves at home here." Martin smiled.

Casey leaped up from the couch spilling parts of Karen's journal on the floor. "I'm sorry. I just got caught up in your sister's journal" Casey stammered out of breath leaning over to pick up some of the pages. Instantly Casey felt a sense of guilt for prying into Karen's personal journal. Standing up she offered the pages to Martin to read.

As Martin looks over the pages, Casey begins to explain, "she's been finding young abused children and giving them to better more loving parents. She is on a mission to save the children." Casey realized how unbelievable this was as she voiced the words aloud. "Of course it is not that simple." Casey starts finding her courage again. "She has a contact who kidnaps the kids, or targets as she refers to the kids, and then sells them to a more deserving family." Casey waits to let this sink in and to see how much Martin already knows. Martin shows no recognition as he flips through the pages faster. "She justifies the selling to help fund her 'mission of mercy,' as she calls it." Again pausing to see the reaction and getting none she continues much softer. "She believed she was saving these children, but then she learned that some were just sold to the highest bidder. Some were not abused kids at all just young girls being sold for God knows what." Martin stared at Casey directly with a pleading look to help him understand. "She decided to cut ties with her connection and save the kids herself, she started with Alyssa Rowe. That's when it all went bad."

"Who was her contact?" Martin asked almost dreading the answer.

"Someone she refers to as LEV or L-E-V, I don't know. I been searching her journals for more information, but that is all she seems to write."

Martin's face hardens at the name of the contact. Holding onto the papers he looks at Casey and says, "You should go now. You got what you wanted. You got your answers."

Stunned by the sudden change of hospitality Casey fires back, "I don't know who her contact is or what happened this time with Alyssa Rowe."

"You don't need to know her contact and trust me you *DON'T WANT TO KNOW.*" Martin states, raising his voice. "Go home, Cassandra and don't look back. Go live your life."

"Come off it, Martin! People are dying around me. What's to say I am not next?" Casey yells back. "I can't just leave pretending I don't know what I know. I can't just leave that little girl out there away from her sister, mother, and the rest of her family."

Martin threw his hands up in exasperation, "what would you have me do?"

"You know who her contact is. I saw it on your face. Get that little girl home. I will take care of the rest."

Martin grabbed her by the shoulder and gave her a shake, "I do this you then you have to promise me something." Casey nearly fell into his arms at his touch. "Cassandra, I am not kidding. You have to swear to me that you will run away. You have to swear that you will go so far away no one will ever find you. You do that for me and I will get that little girl home. Swear it." Martin held her at arm's length looking deep into her eyes.

Martin knew something that Casey didn't and his tone told her to just trust him. "I swear." She promised lowering her head in defeat.

"Now go. Take your family and go."

Casey picked up her purse and started walking to the door. Mani waited for her and she turned back to look at Martin. "Martin, I never stopped loving you. That's not why I left." Casey started to explain.

"Cassandra, please...It nearly killed me the last time you left and now I am sending you away. Please don't tell me you love me."

Casey nodded and turned back to Mani. The tears rolling down her face. Her throat burned and she did not dare say another word. She got into the car as Mani held the door open for her. Sitting in the car she waited for Mani to drive away. Mani said nothing as he drove her to the airport.

CHAPTER SIXTY-SIX

Casey sat at the gate staring out the window at the airplanes. She reviewed what she had learned. She thought about all those children and wondered what had gone so wrong that got Karen killed. Seeing Martin had been so much harder than she had ever imagined. She forced herself to think about Tom and Georgia. Martin said she needed to run. What did he know that he refused to share with her? The thought of running again made every fiber of her being scream in protest, but what could she do. She had not talked with Tom since Tom dropped her off at the house.

Casey dialed Max, "Who has the power to shut down an FBI investigation?" She blurted before Max could identify himself.

Pause, "No one, not even the President of the United States.

"So how did the Alyssa Rowe case get shut down?"

Tapping his pen on the side of his forehead, Max thought about the chain of events that removed this case from them. "It was determined to be local law enforcement jurisdiction. If the case is not federal jurisdiction, but then the case is ongoing with a different team leading the investigation." Max said. *And an Act of Congress!* "The case file ended up at Capitol Hill, maybe it was an Act of Congress." Voicing his thoughts about this case for the first time.

"When you say 'Act of Congress' what do you mean by

that? Do you mean the entire congress or could it be done by a member of congress?"

"Technically, an Act of Congress is just that and it would require a vote by the entire congress, both house and senate, but the reality is any member can threaten an Act of Congress and pretty much get the same results. Your turn, tell me why you are asking."

"Senator Jane Schmidt is all over Karen's journals. Senator Jane Schmidt is a client of Karen's. What did you tell me about coincidences?"

"What kind of client? And I said there are no coincidences."

"The Senator *bought* a baby girl from Karen." Casey deliberately stated each word as she spoke.

"Holy Fuck!" Max exclaims. "Like I said there are no coincidences." Max holds the receiver at arms distance to take this all in. Taking a deep breath he puts the receiver back to his face. "As Tim used to say where there's smoke, there's fire."

"What I got us is a forest fire of smoke. See you soon." Casey hung up before Max could respond. Casey turned off her phone because she was done talking at the moment. She needed to think.

CHAPTER SIXTY-SEVEN

Max sat at his desk drumming his fingers still holding the receiver from when Casey called. He remembered the surprise that the case file had been sent to Capitol Hill. That had been a first in his career and he checked around, no one ever heard of a case being transferred to The Hill. Everything is starting to makes sense. *Damn! I wish Tim were here.* Now, Max understood the who and the why behind all of this, but not quite enough to make an arrest. Max called Senator Schmidt's office and asked to speak with the Senator herself, official business. The Senator came on the line and Max asked to meet face to face to discuss the Alyssa Rowe case. He waited to see if he could hear a reaction. He debated about stating the nature of the meeting, but thought it would be worth hearing any reaction to the name. He got his reaction all right, a distinct sucking in of air at the mention of Alyssa Rowe.

The Senator's Aide informed Max that the Senator was out of the State until next week. Max said that was fine, and he would pick a time then. Max hung up the phone with a smile on his face. He knew that he had stirred up something, and now he would wait and see what happened next.

Max grabbed his jacket off the back of his chair and

headed to the coffee shop on the corner. Whistling to himself, he jogged across the street and into the coffee shop. Max grabbed a booth by the window and waited for the server. As he waited, he thought about his friend Tim. He could not believe that this one case had caused so much destruction. The full impact of the casualties had yet to sink in. Soon Max would be crippled with grief and ask for time off. This had happened in the past when he worked the office in Philadelphia. Max laughed ironically to that thought, the whole reason I am in Maine is because I did not want to deal with such human travesty. Humans can be so cruel and evil with the same motive every time, money. It always comes down to the money.

"Hey, where is your partner in crime?" the familiar voice of the server asked as she reached the table.

"He died the other day in a car accident." Max blurted without thinking of the impact of his statement.

"Oh My God, I am so sorry." Tears welled up in the server's eyes, and she turned and left the table. A moment later she returned with coffee and slice of apple pie. "On the house, sweetie. Sorry for your loss."

Tim would get a kick out the free pie over his death.

Max figured that Casey must have e-mailed the journals by now, so he gulped the last of his coffee and stood up. He dropped a couple dollars on the table and waved farewell to the server. "Thanks, the pie was stupendous?" Blowing a kiss into the air.

Max was eager to get back to his computer and start going through the journals that Casey sent, that he did not take care crossing the street. He sensed rather than heard the vehicle accelerate to hit him. Max hit with such an impact that his body was lifted up over the hood and into the windshield and continued over the top of the vehicle. Max hit the pavement with a bounce and then laid still. He could only glimpse the car that hit him, a green sports utility vehicle, before he lost consciousness.

CHAPTER SIXTY-EIGHT

As soon as Casey landed in Bangor she drove over to the federal building to check in with Max. With Tom and Georgia safe in Canada, she really did not have anywhere else to go. *The sooner with solve this the sooner I get to return to my life.* Casey said hopefully to herself knowing that her life would never be normal.

Casey quickly checked in at the front desk, already familiar she was greeted with a smile and nod. Riding the elevator to the third floor, Casey considered whether to tell Max that she had asked Martin to get the little girl back. She made the decision to hold back. Martin had helped enough and she needed to keep him out of law enforcement's radar. *Who am I kidding he must be the center of countless investigations.* Casey laughed at her own joke.

The elevator door opened and Casey began to walk towards the conference room when the receptionist intercepted her. "Ms. Baker, if you would mind having a seat in the waiting area. I'll get someone to help you." The receptionist pointed to a couch in the front entry and hurried down the hall.

Casey retreated to the couch with a pit of dread in her belly. *This is the reaction I got when Agent Thibodeau was killed.* She was too nervous to sit so she rocked back and forth on her heels, the same motion she used to calm Georgia down when she was just a baby. The rocking did not have the same effect on Casey as it did for Georgia, which was good considering it usually made Georgia fall asleep.

A young man walked up to her with his hand outstretched a good 3 yards before reaching Casey. Casey just stared at the hand trying to decipher what he was telling her, but her anxiety was so high that she could not make out a single word. The man reached her and touched her hand and clasped it with both hands and drew her down to the couch.

Speaking slowly and deliberately, the man introduced himself, "I'm Sam. I work with Max." Pausing to check for understanding, he continued. "There has been an accident and Max is…"

Casey gasps, "Oh, no not Max too." She cried burring her head in her hands.

"Max is in the hospital. He was hit by a hit and run driver this morning and taken to Eastern Maine Medical. It's serious, but he is going to make a full recovery."

Casey burst into tears as she realized how scared she was that Max was dead too. She became hysterical as she sobbed and sobbed. She always lost control when everything was okay and never during in the middle of a crisis. The man put his arm around her until she stopped crying. She looked up and felt her face flush with embarrassment. "I'm sorry. It's been a long couple of days. I normally don't fall apart like this." She accepted his handkerchief and dabbed her eyes and nose. She thought she was the only one who kept handkerchiefs anymore.

He smile was kind and sympathetic. "Like I said, Max is fine he is in Eastern Maine Medical and you can go and see him."

Casey stood and started to hand back the handkerchief back, but David just waved it away indicating for her to keep it. "Would you mind going over your findings before you go see Max?" He looked expectantly at her.

"I want to see Max first, but I'll come back as soon as I see for myself." Casey said as confidently as she could. Her information was for Max and Max alone, after that she was *outta here!*

CHAPTER SIXTY-NINE

Casey drove the couple of blocks to Eastern Maine Medical Center and parked in the parking garage. *Tom's last colonoscopy was here.* Casey thought as she entered the front doors of the hospital. *How normal life had been then, was that only a few months ago?* Casey thought with incredulity shaking her head back and forth. Casey called the hospital en route identifying herself as his sister. Casey knew that the hospital was reluctant to give out any information to anyone who is not part of the immediate family. The operator transferred her to a nurse who told her Max was in critical condition, but the doctors felt optimistic on his chances of a full recovery.

Casey was not prepared to see how banged up he was. The nurse finished taking his vitals as Casey entered. "He's been sedated so don't be surprised if he falls asleep on you." She said and then she was gone. Casey shut the door and pulled a chair up to his bed.

Casey regaled all that she had learned from Karen's journals. Max expressed surprise and then surprised that after all these years with the Bureau that he could even be surprised. He was so happy to see Casey that he could not help smiling and smiling hurt.

"I did a lot of thinking on the plane ride here. I think LEV is the same Lev Odessa you guys were talking about. I guess the only to find Alyssa is through the Odessa Family." Casey said thinking out loud. *That made the most sense, Martin had been visibly shaken at the mention of L-E-V and his immediate reaction was to tell me to run. The Russian Mafia would have that impact. Very little scared Martin, they did.* Casey kept all these thoughts to herself.

"No can do. They are some seriously dangerous people, and they will not talk to the cops. These guys kill judges without batting an eye. Promise me that you will not even try and talk to him."

Casey smiled sweetly and changed the subject, "When are they letting you go home?"

"They really don't know yet. I guess I am lucky to be alive."

"Did you at least get a look at the guy considering you did hit the windshield?" Casey is poking fun.

"You'd think that wouldn't you? But not me, all I got was it was a green SUV"

Casey stopped laughing, "I saw a green SUV in Redwood the day Sally was killed." Casey began to wring her hands, that sixth sense was telling her this was no coincidence.

"Casey, there have to be thousands of green SUV in the Bangor area alone. Of course, you saw a green SUV in Redwood, probably see them all the time."

Casey gave a nervous chuckle, "You are so right." Not convinced, changing the subject Casey said. "Let me go so you can get some sleep. Don't you have a family to come and bug you?" Casey realized that she knew virtually nothing personal about this man that she felt such a strong kinship with.

"Nope, just a helpless bachelor."

"In that case, I'll stop by tomorrow to see how you're getting along." Casey patted his leg and left the room.

As she stepped into the hallway, she notices a man step quickly into the stairwell. His movement drew her attention as if he was reacting to her. Casey shook her head and headed for the elevators. She parked in the parking garage near the front entrance to the hospital. She was considering her next step. She needed to talk with Senator Schmidt, but how can she get in to see the Senator, any senator? She saw the man walking in front of her, and she stopped dead in her tracks. That gait is the same gait of the man who shot Sally. Casey took out her phone and snapped video of the man walking in front of her. She slipped into the hospital gift shop and continued to videotape the man as he exited the building. He must have sensed that she was videotaping because he turned around just as Casey ducked inside the shop, but Casey was confident he did not see her.

Casey watched the video she made and was certain this was the man who walked away from the Moose Pub Café with the rifle case. Casey was somewhat of an expert in human gait. As a child, Casey refused to wear her glasses. Unable to see people's faces she became very good at recognizing their unique pattern of movement. She found that each person's walk, sway, and posture was as unique as a fingerprint. Casey looked at the video she shot to be sure. No question, this is him. She looked out the gift shop window, but he was gone. Casey snapped a still of the man's face and sent it to Tom and texted, "Is this the guy in the green suburban?"

CHAPTER SEVENTY

David did not see Casey walk in because he was so engrossed with his own investigation. Casey cleared her throat getting David's attention. "Can I help you?" He asked taking her all in, *she is really nervous about something.* David was unsure how to respond to her nervous behavior and had half a mind to call security.

"I need to speak with Senator Schmidt," Casey said as firmly as she could. She was exhausted and not really confident she could just walk in and actually see the Senator.

"Do you have an appointment?"

"No, but it's important. Is she here?"

"No, she is not in this office today." David intentionally kept it brief not giving any indication of when the Senator would be available.

"Do you have some way to contact her to arrange a meeting?" Casey asked with a hint of desperation creeping into her voice. She was so tired and she had come so far, in both distance and emotions.

"Maybe if you tell me what this is about, I might be able to help you," David said softening to this woman's obvious emotional distress.

"It has to do with Alyssa Rowe and my dear friend Sally Thornton."

David visibly stiffened at the mention of the names.

Casey caught the subtle change and raised her eyebrows

questioning the assistant. Casey lean forward and almost whispered a prayer, "can you help me?" she begged.

"I can get you in contact with her people that schedule the appointments, but she is scheduled out way into next year." David said aloud as if someone was listening and got up and motioned Casey into the inner conference room. David put a *Do Not Disturb* sign on the outer office door and switched the phones to the switchboard telling them he was taking his break.

Casey walked in the indicated direction and entered a room with a large conference table with at least a dozen chairs. On the far side of the room was a window. She walked towards the window and could see her car in the far parking lot. She sat down in a seat where she could continue to see her car. David reached his hand out and said, "I'm David Turner, and I work for Senator Jane Schmidt."

"Casey Baker, I hope it is good to meet you."

"It's really hard actually to meet with the Senator. Some people wait months just to have five minutes. Something tells me you don't have months to wait and that you will need more than five minutes. I work for her and I hardly ever see her. Maybe if we go over everything I can pass it onto her and then we'll see." David's voice was sincere and reassuring.

"Okay, but just so you know, everyone who gets involved and starts poking around is dead except for me." Casey looks David right in the eye to read his reaction to this. David does seem to be concerned, why is that? "Are you still willing to go over all of this?"

"I am willing and I got involved the minute you walked into the office.

Casey walked David through the whole story from the abduction of Alyssa Rowe, to her friend's accident, Agent Thibodeau's accident, Karen's accident, and so forth. The involvement of the Odessa Family complicates everything. They are here in this country and yet they live by a separate code. Even local law enforcement is afraid to approach them. In this day an age, they are "untouchable". David listens jots down a few notes here and there, but does not add anything to the monolog.

"Now that brings me to Senator Schmidt and what I've learned." Casey inhales deeply before continuing. "She used her office to kill the investigation of Alyssa Rowe. That seemed so odd until you find out that her campaign is financed through a certain law firm that is laundering money for the Odessa Family of Brighton Beach, New York. What I don't get is why not let law enforcement run its investigation and have the case go cold all on its own?"

"Is that it?" David speaks for the first time in over an hour.

"This attorney, Jeff Petersen of Wally, Habermash, and Frederickson, is at the center of everything. He was Karen Tanneger's attorney, Andy Morrell's attorney, and controls the finances for Senator Schmidt's campaign. They also represent the Odessa Family, who is involved in all kind of nefarious acts, including human trafficking. That's quite a bit, and it's more than enough to destroy the Senator's career."

"What role do you think the Senator played in all this?" David asked incredulous.

"I don't know. The Odessa Family is the likely the muscle, but as I said they are insulated, and I don't think that a few hayseeds from Maine are going to be much concern to them. You tell me, looking at the whole picture. Who has the most to lose if the truth about Alyssa were to come out?"

David gulped some air and said deadpan, "Senator Jane Schmidt. A scandal like this would be political suicide." Did David just kiss his job good-bye? That would depend on how the Senator responded.

"What do we do now?" Casey asked staring out the window. She saw someone jogging in the parking lot by her car. The movement is familiar, but hard to know when a person is running. The style is not similar to when a person walks.

"I need some time to get my head straight, but I promise you that I will talk to the Senator and get a feel of what needs to happen. There is no way that she is behind the accidents, so no fear there. I will contact you when I have more information even if my answer is no comment. What is the best number to reach you?"

Feeling dismissed Casey scribbled her cell phone number on the back of one of the Senator's business cards and got up to leave. As she stepped into the hall, she turned and said, "Hey, by the way, Thank you. If I don't see you again, I wanted you to know I appreciate all of this."

Casey closed the door and walked down the hall. As she approached the elevators, she decided to take the stairs. Her mind was a whirl with thoughts, and she needed the activity. The staircase was a large rectangular spiral staircase where you could see all the way to the bottom. Casey spotted the man from the hospital walking away from the bottom steps. In a panic, Casey stepped back from the railing and flattens herself against the stairway wall. Casey creeps back up the stairs and enters the hallway. She considers returning to the Senator's office, but at this point she does not know who to trust. She sees a public bathroom and ducks inside. She is pleased to find an old fashion sitting area inside, reflecting the age of the building, but honestly right now she is grateful. She sits on the vinyl couch and ponders her next move. She can't exactly walk to her car since that is most likely where the man is. She is reminded that there are no coincidences. She saw that guy today in the hospital and now here two hours away. She is positive that it is the same guy that shot Sally. Casey gets out her phone and watches the videotape again to be sure. *Yep, that's him.*

CHAPTER
SEVENTY-ONE

David misses Casey the minute she walks out of the office and is tempted to follow her out. He has her number, maybe he should call her and ask her to dinner. *Everyone has to eat, right?* David begins to justify that since both of them are waiting on the Senator why not wait together? Say, over dinner? David knows better and does not act on his wishful thinking. Pushing the thoughts away, he makes a much dreaded call to the Senator.

Placing a call to Senator Schmidt's private line, David is surprised when the call goes straight to voice mail. "Senator, this is David Turner in Augusta. I had an interesting visitor today. I don't know if she is a nut job, but I didn't get that impression..." Pause..."She uhm," David clears his throat before continuing," made a lot of damning accusations about you and the Alyssa Rowe case. I don't know what she has in terms of evidence, but her story is pretty convincing. She wants to speak directly to you. I told her that it was unlikely, considering your schedule. She went over all the details with me, and well..." Another pause, "it's bad. If this story got leaked it could be really bad, in my opinion. She told me that you are connected to organized crime. Call me and tell me what to do."

David had no idea what to expect next. He knew the

message was blunt, but he wanted to get some kind of immediate response. All those names of people he never met, but he had seen the same list of names on the Senator's computer. He might just get a call saying he was fired or maybe nothing. David crossed his fingers and hoped beyond hope that none of this was true. He really liked the Senator, and this is the kind of stuff that people go to jail for, forget ruined careers.

David waited around the office an extra half hour hoping the Senator would call him back or that girl Casey would come back, but neither happened. He knew the Senator could reach him whether he was at the office or not and decided to head home. David exited the capitol building nearest where his car was park, like he did every other day. David was smiling to himself thinking about the girl. *Probably some nut job,* David thought trying to dissuade himself of thinking of her. The sun was still shining bright as David exited the building, he paused to inhale the fresh air deeply and take in the beautiful day, and the weather was perfect, clear and bright with no humidity. David removed his sport's coat as he stepped off the curb to cross the street and head for his car.

David could hear someone calling his name and turns to look. It was that girl from the office, Casey, he turned towards her voice and smiled not looking at where he was going. David never saw the car that accelerated to run him over. David's last thoughts were how good the sun feels and how lucky he is to have that girl here, chasing after him. Maybe everything will be all right.

CHAPTER SEVENTY-TWO

The man had been called in to handle the Aide situation. He had bugged the home and office, phone and computer. He had been listening to the goings on in this kid's life for a few days now, but this kid was boring. There was no way he was blackmailing the Senator and whatever he "knew" amounted to nothing, because he did not know what he knew, until today. The phones, computers and offices were tracked and monitored by sophisticated software that was designed to send a signal if certain names were used in conversation. So far, none of triggers had gone off until just now. And all of the triggers had gone off. Some outside visitor had shown up demanding to speak with the Senator. Somehow she had pieced together a lot of the story and put the Senator at the heart of it. The man heard every word of David phone message to the Senator. In fact, the man heard every word of his conversation with Casey.

The man had started keeping tabs on David when he was first suspected of blackmailing the Senator. That turned out to be a fluke where he saw a message meant for the Senator and wrote it down. But the woman today, Casey Baker as she had introduced herself, she was *unexpected*. The man did not know that someone outside of law enforcement was investigating. He had to give it to the amateur sleuth, she pretty much nailed it. The only piece missing was the why the Senator was involved. It had nothing to do with the money. Money is nice, but it is not what motivates the Senator.

It seems I had a witness. The man who prided himself on being meticulous and careful smiled at the thought of a worthy challenge. *She may know I exist, but she certainly does not know who I am.* The man smiled again as he waited for David to leave the building. *I am going to have so much fun taking care of the girl.*

The man brought his attention to the task at hand, David Turner. David actually could ID him, but he just didn't know it. This latest encounter made David a threat, David is getting too close to the truth. It will not take him long to connect the dots. The kid is not stupid. It's a shame too, he's a good kid, smart. For the first time in his life, the man was tempted to let this kid go, but he knows that before long the kid would put it all together and that couldn't be allowed to happen.

Here he comes. The man glanced at the clock on his dash. *He's a little later than usual. Unlike the rest of the world, this kid leaves when his work is done not when the clock tells him. You have to respect that kind of work ethic.* The man starts the car and pulls away from the curb slowly keeping David in his sights. He spots David at the crosswalk getting ready to cross with the light. As luck would have it, he is alone in the cross walk so no collateral damage. The light changes and the man in the green Suburban gently accelerates towards David. David steps into traffic and pauses to look behind him. The man follows David's gaze towards the door of the building, but cannot see what David sees. The man hits David with enough of an impact to force him down on the pavement and then turns the vehicle slightly to runs him over with the back wheels. David's lifeless body slides under the vehicle and the man can feel and hear the back wheel roll over the body. The man continues his drive looking back for any signs of life, but nothing. He sees someone run from the building out to David's side. The man turns right at the next corner and doubles back. He wants to make sure that David is

Mary Jane Carter

dead.

CHAPTER SEVENTY-THREE

C asey feels the vibration of her phone indicating a text message. It's from Tom. She hits the icon and reads the one word, "yes". Casey responds, "are you sure?" Tom text back, "yes." Casey knew it. Sure that Tom had a million questions for her she eases his mind by texting, "I'm OK." Tom knows better than to bombard her with questions, he would have to wait until she was ready. Casey peeks out the bathroom door and sees the halls quiet. She walks down the hall back towards the Senator's office, but changes her mind. Feeling more secure in a public building Casey goes to the information desk and asks if there is a cafeteria in the building. The attendant tells her the cafeteria is in the basement. This time Casey takes the elevator to the basement floor and follows the signs to the cafeteria.

The cafeteria looks like a school cafeteria, linoleum tile floors standard tables with plastic chairs. *The food looks as appealing as a high school cafeteria too.* Casey takes a piece of cheery pie and fills a Styrofoam cup with coffee adding in two small creamers and two packets of sugar. The disinterested cashier rings up her total coming to $4.95. *You got to be kidding me.* Casey fishes a five-dollar bill out of her pocket and gives it to the cashier leaving the nickel change. Casey finds a seat in the corner facing the entrance. Taking a sip of the coffee, Casey grimaces at the bitterness even with the cream and sugar. *This shit taste like its been brewing all month!* Casey sits quietly eating her pie and drinking her coffee, watching the door to the cafeteria.

Casey does not know how long she has been sitting in the cafeteria, but the casher is packing up and closing up shop the day. Casey takes her pie plate over to the dish area and drops her half-empty coffee cup in the garbage. Taking the elevator to the ground floor, Casey walks into the main lobby of the building. The place is pretty dead and she sees on the clock in the main hall that it is almost 5:30 pm. *Day must end at five.* The attendant at the information desk is gone and replaced by a guard, rent-a-cop deal. She walks over to the security guard and asks how much longer they keep the building open. He tells her the doors are already locked coming in, but she can exit when she is ready.

Casey moves to the front door and looks out at the parking lot. She can see her car alone in a sea of parking lot. There are still a few cars left, but most of them are gone. She doesn't see anyone hanging around waiting. She does not see the man. She is almost certain that it was him she saw earlier by her car now that Tom confirmed her fears. She is so edgy and jumpy she feels like jumping out of her skin, she shouldn't have had the cup of coffee. She sees David get off the elevator and moves to the side behind a pillar to avoid him. She is half tempted to walk out with him, but if she has learned anything at this point in her life the only one you can truly trust is yourself.

Casey gives David a few moments and makes her way to the parking lot. She sees the green Suburban coming down the street. The passenger side headlight is damaged reminding her of the car she saw in Redwood. The Suburban is going fast and is speeding up. Casey looks down the street and sees David waiting for the light to change.

"Oh my God!" Casey starts running for the exit screaming for David, David looks up and sees her and smiles. The green Suburban slams right into him his body disappearing under the car. The car keeps going and disappears down the street.

Casey sprints out to where David lays on the ground screaming for help from anyone who will listen. Casey kneels by David's body, but she knows it is too late. She begins to wail and scream, rocking back and forth. She has not felt such intense fear and panic since that day in Bogota. "Oh God, help me Oh God" she keeps repeating over and over. *When is this nightmare going to end? I am surrounded by death and destruction.*

A small crowd gathers, and someone helps Casey back inside and sits her on a bench in the lobby. Someone hands her a paper cup with water. They ask her what she saw. Did you see the driver? No. Did you see the car? Not really, it was green. I was trying to help, but it was too late. Can we call some one to come get you? No, I just want to go home. They let her leave asking her to call the next day to give a statement.

The fresh air perks up her senses and she walks to her car. The man is gone. But Casey looks around just to be sure. Seeing no sign of the man or the green Suburban, Casey heads for her car. Wondering if she is okay to drive, Casey gets in and starts the car. She wants to get as far away as possible. *Screw the Senator, I am outta here!*

Casey remembers that she saw the man by her car. She pulls over on the side of the car and gets out looking at her car. She drops to the ground to check underneath and spots what she is looking for under the front fender. It is a small loran like tracking device with GPS capabilities. Casey knew all about this little tracking device because her paranoia of Georgia's safety had her researching devices for her kid, in the event she grew up. She saw this same device on the Internet. *If Tom only knew he wouldn't let her hear the end of it.* The device was just less than a square inch and could easily go undetected.

Casey pulled with some force to remove the tracking device. She almost destroyed it, but thought better of it and put it on the seat next to her. Casey got into her car and sped away. She headed for Redwood where her bed and a chance to think waited.

CHAPTER SEVENTY-FOUR

Casey's eyes tear up as she drives, and she is wiping then away with her hand. She lost it today when she saw David get hit. It wasn't the worst scene she had seen, Bogota had been so much worse. Even then she did not fall apart as she did today. She had been hysterical on the street today. Casey Baker did not get hysterical she barely cried. Casey Baker cried at good-byes and sappy movies.

Walking into the front door of her house, Casey felt such sadness. She missed her daughter, her husband, and the life they had been making. She thought about Sally and today. She had been on command mode since Sally was shot, she kept all her feelings at bay and now standing in the entryway of her house all alone everything she had not allowed herself to feel threaten to consume her in this moment.

Walking to the master bath, Casey turned the hot water on for the shower. She removed her clothes and stood looking at herself in the mirror. She was a little worse for wear, but not too shabby given her age. Her face looked sad, eyes swollen and red, nose pink from crying, skin blotchy from stress.

Once in the shower Casey let all her feeling go, and she sobbed until there was nothing left and she could not shed another tear. Casey wrapped a towel around her hair to dry and put on a bathrobe and padded into the bedroom. She curled up on the bed and went to sleep.

Casey opened her eyes and could see that it was early morning. She looked at the chair and saw Martin sitting there. She bolted upright clutching her robe tightly closed at her neck. Martin put his fingers to his lips motioning her to be quiet. He then motioned with his fingers for the two of them to take a walk. Casey held up her hand indicating to wait a moment and opened her wardrobe. She grabbed a pair of jeans, tee shirt, socks, bra, and underwear and disappeared into the bathroom. She reappeared minutes later all dressed and ready to go.

Casey grabs her jacket and puts on her shoes at the door. The sun is shining promising a nice day. Martin follows Casey out of the house and points to a bench down by the lake. Casey nods, and they both start walking down towards the lake.

Martin begins, "I want to thank you for giving me back my sister. I thought I had failed her. I thought I had lost her to the drugs like our mother." Martin's words revealed a depth of sadness that Casey never saw before, "It's messed up what she did, don't get me wrong, but I understand her now better than ever. Neither one of us had the ideal childhood."

Casey just listened. She did not know what to say. Casey shuddered when she thought of all the wasted lives because of this man and the business he was in. This man, who was technically still her husband, was the man she ran away from in fear for her life. Casey could not bring herself to quite pity the man, but she felt his pain.

"I was going to leave you to deal with this mess." Martin began. "I have been so angry with you for so long and I thought, let her deal with these guys." Martin looked down at his hands while Casey sat looking out at the lake. She knew she had hurt him when she left and she really did not know what she could say that would make any of this right. "How could you think I would ever hurt you?" Martin asked grabbing both of her hands and looking her right in the eyes questioning. Casey just looked at him and said nothing. She had nothing to say. She had acted in a manner that she believed was her only option at the time. Martin let go of her hands and continued. "Then Mani showed me my sister's journals you found and I realized you gave me back my sister."

"What are you going to do now?" Casey asked.

"I'm here, aren't I?"

"I don't know what that means? Are you here to drag me back?"

Martin chuckled. "I've known where you have been for a long time. Hell I have always known where you were. I knew when you got married, which by the way is not legal considering. I knew when you had your baby. That should have been my baby. You didn't want me and so, I made the decision to leave you alone."

"You might have told me." Casey thought about all the time she wasted in hiding.

"You did not hear me, I said, I decided to leave you alone. I didn't say I forgave you." Martin said looking straight ahead.

Both were silent for a spell gazing out at the lake.

Casey broke the silence, "I need to find Alyssa."

"Not possible." Was all Martin said, no questions about why or what good would that do.

"I have to find a way. It is the only thing that can make some of this right."

"Do you have any idea how dangerous these guys are? They make the Cartels look like a bunch of spoiled brats. I couldn't keep my sister wasn't safe from them, how do you think I can keep you safe?" his temper flaring.

"I didn't ask you to." Casey shot back.

"Right, and I am here for my health." Laced with sarcasm, Martin stared at Casey.

'I have to try. I'm getting the fact that no one will be arrested. No one will pay. I don't like it. But that little girl is out there, and she belongs with her family." Casey pleaded.

"You really think she is better off with her family?"

"I believe that we all have a right to the truth. I can't go so far as to say she is better off with her family. She has a sister who desperately wants her back. You of all people can understand that."

Martin was pensive and looked out at the lake. Casey knew that he was giving her request real consideration, so she let her words sink in and bided her time.

Finally, Martin spoke, "Here is the deal. I will make inquiries. I will see what I can find out and I will share that information with you. You will accept what I find out and leave it alone. You realize that you cannot stay here. You know too much, and you are not safe. These are bad people with no morals. They are motivated by money, which could work for you. So long as you do not pose a threat to their income you should be okay. If you disappear from here and keep your mouth shut you and your family will have a chance."

"Tell me why did they kill Karen?"

"Karen made the connection between Alyssa Rowe and human trafficking. My sister Karen realized that when she set up to abduct the kids, these guys also took the mothers and trafficked them as sex-slaves. It is one of the reasons no one noticed the missing children. No one around to report them missing. She threatened to end the operation and like I said these guys are motivated by money and she threaten their source of income."

"Wow," Casey whistled the word, it was all she could think to say. The deeper you go the darker it gets.

CHAPTER
SEVENTY-FIVE

Martin leaves to find out what he can about Alyssa without alerting too much attention. Casey decides to busy herself by creating a record of the events. She sits down at her computer and types up the whole story as far as she knows it. She creates a chart of everyone involved, how they are involved, how the information is known to be true, and if the information is verified. When she is all done she prints out four copies, one for the Boston Globe, one for the New York Times, one for the Washington Post, and one for the FBI. Stuffing the accounts in manila envelopes, she goggles the addresses and quickly addresses each envelop. She uses the sender's address as the return address so no matter what the package will be delivered.

That task accomplished, Casey reaches for the phone and calls Tom.

"It's almost done. I'll fill you in when I get there. Is there anything you want me to bring from the house?" Casey does not want to tell him over the phone that we can't return to the house.

"Just you, in one piece," Tom states affirmatively. "I have someone here that wants to talk to you."

"Mom Mom I miss you! We went to a restaurant." Georgia

sings into the phone.

"I miss you too. What did you eat?" Casey heart swells at the sound of her little girl.

"Pancakes the biggest pancake in the whole world."

"Really! The biggest in the whole world? Were they good?"

"The best in the whole world. I miss you mommy." Georgia started to whine.

"I love you. Kiss Kiss." Casey kissed into the phone.

"I love you too. When are you coming home?"

"Soon sweetie, I promise." Tears poured down Casey's face. Casey was becoming such a sap.

"Bye Mom Mom."

"You Okay," Tom asked getting back on the phone.

"I will be. See you soon."

"Love you, be careful."

"Always." Casey disconnected the line.

CHAPTER SEVENTY-SIX

The drive to Eastern Maine Medical took just under two hours. The distance was exactly eighty miles. The drive gave Casey a lot of time to think about her last few days. She knew that Martin would find Alyssa, it wasn't in him to fail.

Casey thought about Alyssa and her future if when they find her. Rusty Rowe was in no condition to raise a child. Casey had only met her once at the open house and even then Rusty could not show up sober. Martin question about whether Alyssa would be better off with her family began to haunt Casey. *What if Alyssa is better off?* Andy, her own father, sold her, his own flesh and blood for money. There was Theresa, but Theresa was just a kid herself. Was Theresa ready to raise her baby sister? There were so many uncertainties, and Casey did not know what to do. In her heart she knew was that the truth was always the best way to go, in the end the truth always has a way of coming out and then what. This is one of those truths that is too much. Casey thought about the Senator's child. What will happen when she learns that her mother bought her? Casey prayed she was doing the right thing and felt strongly that in this moment she needed to have faith that everything happens for a purpose even her being in the middle of this mess. Chanting in her head, *things have a way of working out the way they should,* Casey drove the rest of the way into town.

Getting out of her car in the parking garage, Casey saw the tracking device. "Shit!" She muttered to herself. She forgot about it and that man could find her, Max, Martin. She picked up the device and walked to the next floor of the parking garage. She found a car, same make and model as hers and put the device on the front bumper. *That should buy her enough time to get out of town.*

Max had been moved to a private room on the third floor. This was a great sign that he was making a full recovery. There was one security guard posted at his door, and he was hesitant to let her in to see Max.

"Only family and those on the list."

"He has no family and I should be on the list. Go tell him its me, Casey Baker." The guard reluctantly poked his head in and asked if he wanted to see a "Casey Baker." Casey could not hear the response, but the guard step aside and waved her in. No apologies or pardons, just a nasty stare as if Casey had insulted him. Casey stuck her tongue out at him as she entered.

"Hey, Max you're looking better."

"Thanks, tell me what's up?"

"Tell me why the guard? You in trouble?"

"No, they think this was no accident."

"Really?," Casey said sarcastically. "What was their first clue, the lack of tire marks on the road or the tire marks on your face?"

Max laughed, "Don't make me laugh it hurts too much."

Casey filled Max in on her meeting with the Senator's Aide and the plan to confront the Senator. Casey did not tell Max about being followed, her visit with El Guapo, or the press releases she had prepared and was planning on mailing on her way out of town. "Is there any way that the FBI can locate Alyssa now that you know what happened to her?"

"It's a long shot. People with too much to lose would have to come forward and in my experience that does not happen.

Take comfort that she is alive, safe, and obviously well loved."

Casey had already expected the limits of the FBI, but she nodded and smiled. "I was afraid of that and I do take comfort that she is with someone who really wanted her. This is all in your hands now. I don't know if you have enough to prosecute Andy, but as for me, I'm out."

"Understood," Max said knowing that he was going to miss Casey.

"No offense, but hope I don't see you again." Casey laughed, leans over and kissed him on the cheek. "So long FBI man." With that Casey left.

CHAPTER SEVENTY-SEVEN

On the way back from the hospital, Casey stopped and mailed her packages, one to the Boston Globe, one to the New York Times, one to the Washington Post, and one to the Chicago Tribune. She thought about sending one to Langley, but they already knew and she was fairly certain that they weren't not about to take action. She hoped to get some investigative reporter on this it was the only hope of anything being done about this is to expose it. Casey was doubtful that Andy would ever be arrested. There really was no hard evidence, no smoking gun, just Karen's journals and how could anyone really authenticate the veracity of a drug lord's sister's account. Maybe exposing this case will help to solve other missing person cases. Maybe those adoptive parents out there will understand how their children came to be. If there is no demand then, there is no need for supply. Casey chucked to herself, that used to be the Martin's argument, if the Americans wanted coffee as much as they wanted cocaine he's would be dealing in coffee, a simple matter of supply and demand.

Casey pulls into the driveway and sees his car. Her heart is pounding at the thought of seeing him again. All this time she had been terrified of seeing him and now that she has she is terrified to not see him. Martin is sitting on the porch and stands as she approaches.

Waving towards the lake, "Nice view I meant to mention last time, but you distracted me."

"I'm surprised to see you again. I thought if you found anything out you would just call." Casey said abrasively she immediately regretted her tone and wished she could take it back.

Martin bristled, "Do you want my help or not?"

"I'm sorry. That came out all wrong."

"I have an address, the adoptive parents allegedly no nothing of the abduction, but you'd have to live under a rock not to know. That could make them very defensive and possibly dangerous. This is the best that I can do." Martin pulled a piece of paper out of his jacket pocket and handed it Casey.

Casey reached for the paper, but Martin pulled it out of reach and said, "Just so you know this makes us even. After today, you go your way, and I go mine."

Casey's heart hurt hearing those words. "I understand, but just so you know. I never wanted you out of my life, not then not now."

Martin stared at her and held the paper just out of reach. "You have no right to rewrite history. I said I did not forgive you." He retorted angrily.

"I was a stupid student who fell in love with a man, two men as I recall. The one who married me and this one standing in front of me right now." Angry shouts turning into sobs, "I'm sorry I couldn't accept the violence. I'm sorry I couldn't love you enough to ignore your business. Sixty-three people Martin! Sixty-three people are dead because of me. Sixty-three mothers and fathers grieving for their children because I loved you! And lets talk about Ana..." Casey screams turned into sobs as she cried for her long lost daughter. Casey collapse onto the steps of the porch heaving sobs of grief for dreams long ago dead and buried.

Martin sat down next to her and cradled her in his arms, "I thought you hated me Cassandra. I thought you left me because you blamed me for killing Ana. I felt responsible. I hated myself. When you left, I blamed you for all the hate in my life. I wanted my family back." Martin was rocking Casey with tears in his eyes. Casey pressed her back against his chest and let him hold her. They sat like that for a long time just holding onto one another because they both knew that when they let go it would be for the last time.

"I want to buy this house. You're not safe here. You can't stay here with the Odessa Family looking for you and I like it here. If they don't know where you are now, they will. I can't protect you from them, but I can help you hide. I need to know that you are safe. Plus, if you ever need to find me you will know where to look." Martin broke the embrace and handed over the slip of paper.

Casey took the paper the reality of running again hitting her full force, "I want a fair price. I'm not giving this place away." Casey smiled.

Martin laughed, "I'll give you fair market value and not a penny more."   They both laughed, laughter through tears is the best emotion there is.

CHAPTER SEVENTY-EIGHT

Theresa wakes with a splitting headache. She tries to open her eyes, but the little bit of light hurts her eyes. She lays still and rubs her temples with her fingers. She tries to think, where is she? What happened to her? Her mind is a blank. Slowly she realized that her whole body aches. She slowly opens her eyes while continuing to rub her temples. Theresa is lying on a bed in a windowless room. *Think!* She commands herself, but her mind is so fuzzy. She feels funny all over and it is hard to think.

She remembers walking home from school and getting to her house. Her mother was sitting in the front room on a chair. *Oh my God!* Theresa remembers seeing her mother in that chair and then everything goes back. She has hazy memories of people pushing her here and there and yelling at her, but none of it makes sense.

Her eyes are adjusting to the light and she looks around. There is nothing in the room, but the bed she is lying on. There is just a sheet and no covers. Theresa looks down and sees that she is wearing only a black negligee that falls to her mid-thigh. She tries to stand, but she moves too fast. Her head is spinning and she sits back on the bed to stop from falling over. She puts her head down between her knees to stop the room from spinning. *What is wrong with her?* Her whole body aches and she remembers that there were men coming and going out of the room. *They injected her with something that made her feel warm and good.* She is really hungry, confused, and scared out of her wits.

She hears the keys jangle as someone unlocks the door. The doorway if filled with a large male, but the light from behind him makes it impossible to make out his face. Theresa holds her hands up to her eyes to get a better look at the man, but his body overshadows his face. Theresa's heart is pounding and her mouth goes dry. She tries to swallow to speak, but no words come out.

The man's voice booms in broken English, "You're awake? Good. I have some friends that want to meet you." The man moves from the doorway and some more men enter the room. Theresa eyes are wide open as her adrenaline pumps in anticipation. "You be a good girl to my friends, you show them good time."

The man leaves her alone with his friends. Theresa feels like screaming as she knows that these men plan to rape her. All that can escape is a whimper as the first man puts his hand on the side of her face. She stiffens at his touch. He grabs her face hard and shoves his hand up her negligee and inserts his finger inside her. "You like, bitch don't you."

Theresa begins to cry out, "No please stop." But her pleas only make him more aggressive. He pushes her down on the bed and rapes her. When he is finished he says something, but she cannot understand him. Another man injects something into her arm and she feels that familiar warmth and sense of well being. She soon does not care what these men are doing to her as her mind drifts to a better place. She is surprisingly at peace and happy. She barely notices when the men leave and she is all alone. Theresa is surprised at how good she feels and gets why her mother abuses drugs.

After a long while, Theresa is not sure how long, a young girl entered the room carrying a basin of water. Theresa asks, "Where are we?" But the girl does not respond. The girl is young maybe Theresa's age with a lost vacant gaze in her eyes. She approaches the bed and places the basin on floor and sits down next to Theresa. She reaches down and brings up a washcloth and begins to clean Theresa's body. Theresa relaxes and enjoys the feel of warm water on her body as the girl work. Theresa reaches out and grabs the girl's arm, but the girl shrugs it off and continues until she is done. She gets Theresa a fresh negligee and drops in on the bed next to her. Theresa looks at the clean negligee and puts it on. The girl leaves with the dirty negligee and water basin. Theresa relaxes on the bed and is surprised at how good it feels to be clean. The girl returns with a tray of food and leaves it on the floor by the bed. Theresa rolls over on her stomach and looks down at the tray of food and is surprised to find how hungry she is. The tray has some kind of flat bread and meat stew. There are no utensils so Theresa uses the bread to scoop up the stew into her mouth. The food is delicious and Theresa eats the entire plate clean.

Hearing the keys jingle by the door draws Theresa's attention. She looks to see a large man walking in.

"Good you have food." The man with the broken English says.

Theresa is surprise to find she is not afraid of him this time. "Where am I?" She asks.

"Where is of no concern to you. I bought you. You belong to me. "The statement slowly sinks in and Theresa looks horrified. "It's not so bad, you be good to me and I be good to you. You like what we give you, eh?" The man sneers.

"I want to go home!" Theresa starts, but the man interrupts her.

"From now on you speak only when I ask you to speak. Otherwise you are silent. If you cry I will punish you." The man said matter-of-factly.

Theresa wants to cry, but she is afraid of what this man will do to her. She holds herself very still. The man looks her over and waits. He sighs, and says, "you get some rest. We have a very big night tonight with lots of friends to play with." He laughs. On his way out her repeats what he said, "you be a good girl and I will be good to you." The man locks the door and Theresa can hear his foot fading away as he leaves. When she is certain that he is gone she rolls over on her stomach and cries into the mattress to muffle any sounds. She realizes that there is no one who will even come looking for her. She is fairly certain that Rusty was dead the last time she saw her and her grandmother could care less about her. Theresa was all alone and nobody cared or would even notice she is gone. Theresa cried herself to sleep wondering what terrors her new life held for her.

CHAPTER SEVENTY-NINE

With all the misery and misfortune that was going on, Casey felt good about one thing. Casey knew that Martin would find Alyssa and bring her home. Casey wanted to see Theresa and give her the hope that she was certain the kid needed. There is just one thing that Casey needs to do first. Casey stops by the cemetery on her way to visit Theresa Rowe. She finds Sally's grave easy enough considering it is the only freshly dug grave in the place. There is no headstone yet, but she is certain this is Sally's resting spot, no need to ask anyone. The cemetery maintenance man spots her and heads in her direction, but stops when he recognizes her and just smiles and waves. He pauses to wait if there are any questions for him with no indication from Casey he returns to his own work and leaves her alone.

"I don't do funerals, I don't do good-byes, and I guess I am a crappy friend, but I am your friend. I am so sorry for what happened to you, but I want you to know that the world will know about you, what you did. I made sure of it. I don't know if justice will be served, but the world will know." Casey bent down on her hands and knees and planted a watermelon seed on her grave. *Just plant a watermelon on my grave and let the juices slurp through.* It was an old joke between the two of them. They carpool to a conference on time and this song comes on the radio, it was the refrain from an old folk song and both of them could not stop laughing. They had both laughed so hard they about peed in their pants and had to pull the car over. Since that time, when anything got too intense one of them was likely to start singing, "just plant a watermelon on my grave and let the juice slurp through" and everything in the world would become instantly better. "I will miss you." Placing a Hershey's Kiss on the grave in lieu of the traditional stone of remembrance. Casey got up and brushed the dirt off her pants and solemnly walked to her car. Next stop good news.

Casey pulled into Rowe's driveway of the rental house. Casey was glad to see the lights in the front room were on, that meant someone wash home. Casey took a deep breath and got out of the car. She wasn't exactly sure what she was going to say, but she wanted Theresa to have hope. Casey knocked on the door and waited on the front porch. No one came to the door, so Casey pounded on the doorframe with the heel of her hand. There still was no response and Casey could feel a sense of dread. She moved to the window and looked in and could see Rusty sitting in an overstuffed armchair. She knocked on the window, but Rusty didn't move. Casey knocked on the windowpane and called out Rusty's name. "Hello, Rusty Rowe, It's me Casey Baker from the High School." Rusty did not move and Casey instantly knew that something was seriously wrong. Casey tried the front door, but it was locked. *No one locks their doors in Redwood.* She banged on the front door as loud as she could, calling out Rusty's name. Casey shakes on the door handle hoping to jimmy the lock on the door, but it was no use. Casey had a bad feeling about this.

Casey knew the landlord, Bill McKlien, he lived in the house at the end of the driveway about thirty yards away. Casey looked over at Bill's house and saw that he was home. She began running and calling out Bill's name at the same time. Bill stepped out onto his front stoop pulling a sweatshirt down over his head. His face read complete surprised to see Casey running towards him.

Before Bill could respond, Casey burst out, "There something wrong with Rusty. The door is locked and she is sitting in her front room not moving at all!" Casey voice cracked as panic set in. Casey turned and started running back to Rusty's house.

Bill could hear the urgency in her voice and immediately went and got the key for the house and ran after Casey to his other house.

Both panting out of breath, Bill unlocked the front door. The minute they entered the house the stench of rotting flesh hit them. Rusty Rowe was dead and had been for a long time. Casey could see the needle still in her arm. "You stupid stupid bitch." Casey muttered out loud as she takes in the whole scene.

"That's odd." Bill says looking at Rusty.

"What's odd, that a drug addict overdosed!" Casey retorts.

"The needle. It's still in her arm usually they get the dose in before they know it too much. You don't usually see them with a needle sticking out of their arm." Bill rubbed his beard and he thought about what he was looking at.

"What are you saying? Are you saying she was murdered?" Casey looked at Bill. Casey realized that she had no real experience with drug use and Bill did.

"I don't know. Just saying its real odd."

Suddenly she realizes that Theresa is gone. "Where is Theresa?" In a panic she grabbed Bill by the shirt and yelled. "For Christ's sake where the hell is Theresa?" Bill takes in the scene with wide eyes shaking his head back and forth. "Call the police I gotta get out of here." Casey turns on her heels and head to her car. Casey's immediate response is to drive like a bat out of hell, but she sits in her car staring at the front door of the Rowe's shabby rental. The police pull up and Jeff Sanders walks over to her car and knocks on window.

Casey rolls down the window and turns to look at Jeff.

"Hey Casey, want to tell me what's going on?"

Casey points to the house as tears start streaming down her face. "Rusty is dead and Theresa is gone."

Jeff turns to look at the house and then turns to look at her, "Sit tight. I'll be back in a minute." Jeff walks to the house.

She planned on leaving, but sits in her car waiting for Jeff. She knows she cannot leave without creating suspicion. She hopes Jeff will come back and tell her Theresa is on some school fieldtrip or at the game. She needs to know where Theresa is. She needs to know that Theresa is safe. Casey is not going to get what she needs today.

CHAPTER EIGHTY

The man tracks Casey's car to a townhouse in Freeport. He does not see the car, but the townhouse has a single car garage with no outside windows or doors to get in and check on the car. The man is confident that this is the house, the locating device he placed on Casey's car is accurate within six feet.

The townhome is a split-level with stairs leading up and down from the main entrance. The man looks in through the transom and sees no evidence of anyone at home. The man can see today's mail sitting on the floor in front of the mail slot in the door. Looking at the wall to the right of the door is a security keypad and the man is amused that they would bother to put in a security system, but not bother to put up a blind on the front transom. From here he could practically read their mail and with the mail slot he was certain he could retrieve a piece of mail if he wanted.

The man jogged back to his car and settled in to wait for his lady friend to come home. The car was in the garage, so she must have gone for a walk. This was Freeport and there was quite a bit of foot traffic about. His bosses wanted this Casey woman eliminated. The man studied her picture and felt it a shame to kill the bitch when they could easily find a buyer for her. *A good-looking woman like her should fetch a pretty fair price.* Of course, he really did not care one-way or the other. He was paid, and paid well, to take care of the problem however the client saw fit.

The man was getting old, he was getting nostalgic. A part of him admired this Casey woman. She was the first one to ever figure out that he existed. He knew it was only a matter of time before he tracked her down, but still it was fun to actually be in the game with someone who gave him a challenge. He was really going to miss her when she was gone.

A young couple pushing a stroller and walking an excited boxer paused in front of the townhouse. The man bent down and picked up the baby from the carriage and walked up the steps as the woman opened up the door to the house.

What the fuck! The man sitting in the car looked at the couple as they carried the baby inside and the dog ran in between their legs. He sat staring at the door as the man came back out and folded up the carriage and carried up the stairs and inside the front door, closing the door behind him as he entered. The man in the car stared at the closed door on the townhouse unsure of what to do next.

Shit! The man pounded his fist on the dash of his car. Now he was getting angry at this bitch is really getting on his nerves. He walks up to the house and rings the bell. The same young lady he saw on the street answers the door.

"I'm looking for a friend of mine, Casey Baker?" The man asks looking for a reaction.

"No one here by that name. You must have the wrong address." The woman says without any indication that she is hiding something.

"Sorry to bother you." The man says and turns to walk away.

"You might try the visitor's center. Mary Monroe runs it and she knows just about everyone in this town. It's right on the south side of town as you come in from the interstate."

"Thank you. I appreciate your help." The man tipped his hat and walked back to his car. The young woman watched him walk away and shut the door.

The man picked up his phone and texted the message. "I

Mary Jane Carter

lost her."

CHAPTER EIGHTY-ONE

The ambulance arrives and Casey watches her friends Dave and Shanna get out and walk to the back to grab the gurney. Dave waves a friendly hello to Casey and she waves back. Casey waits for them to remove Rusty's body. She watches the friendly faces that walk into the house come out with somber faces.

Casey gets out of the car and stretches her legs. She had been sitting in her car all tense and her legs were now cramping as a result. She rubs the back of her thigh as she waits and watches for Jeff to come out of the house. *There is no way I am going back into that house.* As if hearing her thoughts Jeff appears on the porch and lights up a cigarette. Casey waves him over and he walks in her direction.

"You don't mind if I smoke? Pretty grisly in there." Jeff points his thumb back towards the house like he is hitching a ride.

"No, go for it. What about Theresa?" Casey waves her hand at the cigarette smoke, she hates smoking, but right now her thoughts are with Theresa.

Jeff shakes his head back and forth. "I called the school and she hasn't been there for the past three days." Jeff takes a long drag on his cigarette and watches the smoke as he exhales before continuing. "I got a call in to the Grandmother, maybe she is there. " Jeff did not sound very convincing. As if on cue, his phone rings and Jeff looks at the number, He steps away from Casey as he takes the call stomping his cigarette out on the ground.

Jeff has to inform this woman on the phone that her daughter is dead and her granddaughter might be missing. Casey can hear Jeff talking into the phone, but she cannot make out the words. He looks up at her and shakes his head no. Casey heart skips a beat. *Where could Theresa be?*

Jeff ended his phone conversation and walked over to Casey. His expression was grim.. "The kid isn't at her grandmother's. Actually, that isn't her biological grandmother and she said she really did not know Theresa. It's been over forty-eight hours, so I will call in the FBI. Any other thoughts?" Jeff looked at Casey hoping she might have some leads.

Casey shrugged her shoulders, "She was pretty new and the only person who might know more is Sally but..." Casey could not finish the statement and the thought hung in the air between them.

Jeff nodded and put his hand out to Casey. "If you think of anything just give me a call. I'm going to go talk to Bill and see what he remembers." Jeff rolled his eyes over to where Bill was standing on his front stoop watching the whole scene.

Casey thanked Jeff giving him a hug, she knew he did not have the resources or talent for real detective work, but he would try his best. This was a small town in the middle of nowhere that never saw any major crime. Jeff's biggest criminal acts were high school students drinking in the woods. People did not get murdered in their offices or children sold by and to desperate parents. There were no ties to organized crime here or major drug lords.

The FBI could not find Alyssa how are they going to find Theresa. *If Theresa Rowe is to be found, I am going to have to find her myself.*

CHAPTER EIGHTY-TWO

C asey scours the online newspapers looking for any hint of the material she sent. There was nothing in the Boston Globe until the New York Times and Washington Post ran with the story. The New York Times ran the following headline: *Baby for Sale in Maine Sponsored by Senator June Schmidt.* There was no mention of the Russian connection in the Times. The Washington Post on the other hand lead with all the connections, their headline read; *Maine's Human Trafficking Conspiracy with Ties to Colombian Drug Cartel, Russian Mafia, and Senator Schmidt.* The major television syndicates picked up the story for long enough to destroy Senator Schmidt's career. The newscaster referred to their source as an "unnamed source." Casey made sure that if the press went looking for the source they would find Karen Tanneger. *It was her story to tell, I was just the messe*nger.

Casey reads further and sees the Senator Jane Schmidt had no comment on the story, but did make the decision not to seek re-election next term. Casey chortle, *right and I'm sure one thing had nothing to do with the other.* Casey continued to read about the Senator's tenure in office, her background, family, blah, blah, blah. *A real paramount of integrity, dedication and truth...* The article on the Senator was very flattering in many ways, but the tide of public opinion was being swayed as more and more came out about the amount and source of her campaign finances were released. The words *her adopted daughter Carolyn* jumped out at Casey. *It was about her daughter. The Senator was protecting her daughter.* Casey remembers the initial shock of finding out that the Senator bought her baby. Casey could almost feel sympathy for the Senator. *What wouldn't I do to protect Georgia?*

Opponents of Schmidt, on Capitol Hill, were calling for Senator Schmidt's resignation and demanded that charges be filed for her role in all of this. Schmidt's supporter countered that the problem lies in campaign finance reform. Congress was also demanding a full-blown FBI investigation into all the allegations of baby selling and its ties to organized crime.

Casey places a call to Martin. "Did you read the Times and the Post?"

"You better hope they cannot connect your name to any of this mess." Martin spitted through clenched teeth.

"No way, if they find any trail it will lead them to Karen. It's her story." Casey retorted.

"Great, that's all I need. You know I've got a business to run, and it's not the kind of business that likes publicity!" Martin smiled shaking his head. Maybe having Casey back in his life was not worth the aggravation. No, something was better than nothing.

"The real reason I am calling you is because Theresa Rowe is missing. I found the mother Rusty Rowe dead of an overdose in her house, but no Theresa. Can you see if your friends know where she is?"

"I'll see what I can do, but this is a long shot." Martin rolled his eyes to the ceiling. "Have you ever heard about poking a snake through bars of his cage?"

"I'm not going to poke anyone, you are." Casey smiled. She was glad to have a reason to call Martin. She was glad to have him back in her life. "See what you can do. This kid is all alone in this world, and I'm afraid that she did something stupid like run off or something. I'd like for her to know her sister is at least okay."

CHAPTER EIGHTY-THREE

Casey fills a backpack with some of Georgia favorite stuffed animals. Georgia names all of her friends and each one is her *favorite*. Casey wished she could take them all, but she was concerned about room. *Time to make some new friends.* She walks down the steps of her home for the final time. She is selling the house to Martin for better than market value. If she forgot anything, she can always have Martin ship it later.

Where will you go? Martin had asked her. She told him she did not know. She and Tom would have to decide. I'll let you know where we are when we land. There had been nothing on locating Theresa and Casey begged Martin to keep looking. It was as if Theresa Rowe just vanished into thin air.

Casey felt free for the first time in longer than she could remember. Ironic because according to Martin, she was in more danger than ever before. *These people don't kid around, and they have a penchant for torture.* Casey just could not bring herself to be afraid. She and Tom had always been prepared to bug out. We have new identities ready to go, money in the bank and even more when the sale of the house is finalized. Tom, Georgia, and I will hide in plain sight, and no one will ever find us.

Casey had just decided where they were headed, the

Midwest. If we are going to hide in plain sight, then where better than the Heartland of America? Casey threw the backpack into the back of the car and drove away. This time she was driving to her destination not running away.

Tom and Georgia are playing in the front yard of the B&B when Casey pulls up. Georgia spots her car and starts to run towards her, Tom scoops her up and waits for Casey to park the car. Casey jumps out of the car and starts towards Georgia.

"Put me down Daddy," Georgia wiggles in Tom's arms. He sets Georgia down on her feet, and she takes off running to her mother.

Casey gets down on her knees and opens her arms wide, and her daughter runs into her outstretch arms.

"I missed you so much Mom Mom."

"I missed you too. I love you." Casey lifts Georgia up in her arms, and Tom joins them for a group hug.

"Welcome back. All is good?" Tom asks.

"All is good. Of course, we can't go back to Redwood, and I did make some nasty enemies with the Russian Mob." Casey smiles. "I'll fill you in later. Right at this moment the world is grand."

CHAPTER EIGHTY-FOUR

The man stops his green Suburban on the road and looks down the driveway. He cannot see the house from the road. The man drove down the driveway in Redwood looking for Casey Baker. He does not see her car in the driveway. He stops his SUV and looks around. The door to the house open and two heavily built men step out onto the porch with automatic rifles and look at his direction. The man sits in his car and for the first time he is not sure how to proceed. The guards walk towards the car. The man holds his handgun in his lap.

Rolling down the window as the guards approach the man yells, "I'm looking for Casey Baker?" He asked like he was an old friend.

"No one here with that name." The first guard said.

"Do you know where I can find her?" Redwood is small town and if he got the wrong address they should know where she lives.

"Don't know anyone by that name." The first guard continued, obviously the talker of the two.

"Do you know where I can find her?" The man asked the second guard. The guard was did not answer. He stood in front of the car and motioned with his automatic rifle for the man to leave.

The man got the message loud and clear and backed his car down the driveway. That was his last lead to the whereabouts of Casey Baker. He had never lost a tail in his life, until now. The man drove to the Moose Pub Café and sat in the parking lot. He could start asking folks around here, but with all the press lately he was sure that would rouse suspicion. He drums his fingers on his steering wheel thinking about how he could possibly lose her. Somehow, Casey figured out he existed, but he was still certain she did not know who he was. He texts his boss, "she's gone."

His phone immediately chimes a new text message. "Find her."

The man pulls out of the Moose Pub Café parking lot and heads for home. This case has turned into a missing persons case and he happened to be very good and finding missing people. Casey Baker was on the run, but she is an amateur. She is going to make mistakes. The man settled in liking the idea that he was about to become intimately acquainted with this young Casey Baker. *You win some you lose some, but not me. I don't lose.*

CHAPTER EIGHTY-FIVE

Nikolay Pavlovitch of the famed Odessa Family sat at his desk reading the New York Times. There were a few inaccuracies, but for the most part the reporter had gotten the story correct. There was no mention of the Family's involvement, but given the fall out Nikolay was concern that it was only a matter of time before his family was connected to this. He has spent years building a business and keeping its nature a secret and that woman destroyed all of that in one fell swoop.

His younger brother Mikhail walked in holding a copy of the Washington Post. "You better read this." He said tossing the paper in front of him. The headline said it all: *Maine's Human Trafficking Conspiracy with Ties to Colombian Drug Cartel, Russian Mafia, and Senator Schmidt.*

"Derrmo!" Nikolay pounded his fist on the desk and continued to read the whole article muttering swears. The Post had the whole story and from the tenor of the article, it looked like the beginning of a series of articles into each of the facts. "Do we know where the little cunt is?" He snarled at this brother.

His brother shook his head no. "We had a lead on where she lived, but she was gone before we got there. She is scared maybe she will keep her mouth shut?"

"She was scared enough to do this." Nikolay said waving the Washington Post around. "Find her." He slammed the paper down on his desk.

Mikhail bowed his head and backed out of the office.

CHAPTER EIGHTY-SIX

The story made CNN, which surprised Casey as she watched. She watched the footage of Andy Morrell being escorted out of his house in handcuffs. She watched the footage of reporters outside the Odessa Family Complex in Brighton Beach.

Nancy Grace went on and on about the how the father sold his baby girl for money while the mother was seeking treatment for drug addiction. Casey figured that Nancy must have mention baby for sale a hundred times in less than an hour show. There was no mention of Theresa the older sister and the story of the mother was an accidental overdose. The coroner had ruled Rusty's death an accidental overdose given her long history of drug abuse. Casey knew better. It was like all the other misfortunate accidents that surrounded the entire case. Everyone who died connected to this case was ruled accidental death, even Sally's death was considered a hunting accident. Casey knew that it was due to lack of evidence suggesting otherwise. The press however made an issue out of all the accidents hitting at foul play by suggesting that anyone who learned anything conveniently died. This case was either corrupt or cursed, that was how the press reported the story. Casey knew it was highly unlikely that anyone responsible would really pay for all those hurt, but at least Andy Morrell was going to jail.

The reporters filmed the reunion with Alyssa and

her great-grandmother, Denise Morrell, in Maine. The great-grandmother's story was a sad one. Denise had lost her husband, son, and grandson, but at least she now had her great-granddaughter back. The adoptive parents posed to fight for custody, but then quickly changed their minds. In a flurry of cameras and reporters, the adoptive parents flew with Alyssa to Maine to reunite her with her great-grandmother. The reunion scene made Casey cry. It was the right thing to bring Alyssa home.

Senator Jane Schmidt was not seeking re-election and was not available to comment. The reporters were still camped outside her doors. With no comment from the Senator the reporters began to speculate about the origins of Carolyn's adoption. The Senator held firm in giving no comment and looked like the decision was to wait out the press. Casey knew that there was little if any hard evidence connecting the Senator to the criminal side of this investigation. The Senator was not the first politician to receive campaign contribution from the seedier sources.

One of the news panel had Special Agent Max talking about the FBI's role in this investigation He commented on the process and gave vague, generic scenarios on how he followed the leads. Max talked about the process of tracking leads and interviewing suspects. Max brought up the carnage in this particular case to underscore the ruthlessness of those directly involved. Casey held her breath waiting, but Max did not mention her at all. When the report was over, Casey slowly exhaled. *Thank you,* Max, Casey sent a silent prayer to the gods. She looked around her and saw her daughter playing in the corner and went over to play with her.

EPILOGUE

Casey laughed with glee watching her daughter splash in the waters of Lake Michigan. It felt so good just to laugh with such carefree abandonment. Squeals of laughter roared out of her daughter with each wave crashed into her. *I forgot how much fun waves were. We did not have real wave action on Moose Lake.* Maggie ran up and lifted Georgia high in the air twirling her around provoking and even greater round of laughter from the little girl.

At first, the move was hard on Georgia. Georgia kept asking when she could return to her brown house, but she quickly adjusted to her new life. Georgia was a happy kid, and that was all that mattered. Maine was pretty, but nothing beats the beauty of The Great Lakes. This feels like home. *I am so glad to be home.* The new and improved Casey relaxed at the thought of being *home.*

The word on Theresa was not good, too much time had past since her disappearance. Martin was convinced that Theresa had been sold in the white slave trade most likely to a country with no extradition. Although Martin had told her to leave this alone and to stop seeking, she knew that he would continue the search as if Theresa were his own sister. Casey took comfort in knowing that if Theresa is to be found, Martin will find her and bring her to me.

There was something so reassuring about starting over. Getting used to the idea that she was finally safe, her family was safe, was going to take some time. When you live your life on the edge all the time, everyone and everything is a potential threat. There was so much farmland in this part of the country, hard to believe when you are living on the East Coast, but most of the world's food is grown right here. Casey had always felt a sense of pride that she came from a place that feed most of the world. You don't get too much more down to earth than farming. Casey had been smiling since the arrived. Now she could start living, no fear, and no regret.

Her pocket vibrated signaling a new text coming in: *C. I had a visitor here looking for you. They are seriously pissed off. Not that I care. They are not giving up anytime soon. WATCH YOUR BACK. I happen to be quite found of it. M.*

Out of habit Casey looked around her to see if anyone was watching her. *So much for new beginnings* Casey sighed. Casey was tempted to text him back begging him to take her away, but she didn't. She looked at the phone and finally typed two letters, O K. Despite the new round of worries, she could not help smiling. Martin was back in her life, if only at a distance. *And he still loves me!* Holding the phone tight Casey makes a promise to herself, *it's not over between us, somehow, someway we will find our way back to each other.*

AUTHOR'S NOTE

*T*he issue of human sex trafficking is becoming a real serious problem in the US. The problem is under reported by both the press and the victims, leaving many shocked to learn that this is happening in their backyard. Many of the traffickers are thought to be associated with organized crime, domestic and international. In researching my next book, I encountered a young lady who was abducted right in her own driveway while her mother was inside the house, completely unaware. Her ordeal for next few years would force her into prostitution not more than 10 miles from her family home. In my next book, <u>One by One the Girl Go Missing</u>, we take a closer look at human sex trafficking and our old pal Casey. When Casey learns of her mother's impending death, she is forced to return to Redwood to say her good-byes. Her return triggers a renewed interest in her. While, Casey is making a new life with her husband and young daughter in the safety of the Midwest, she is oblivious to how close she is to the ones she is hiding from. Trying hard to stay out of trouble, and keeping her family safe, trouble always seems to find Casey in the most unexpected places.